THE PRODUCER'S UNLIKELY BRIDE

A CLEAN OPPOSITES ATTRACT ROMANCE

LORANA HOOPES

NOTE FROM THE AUTHOR

I have been so blessed to meet amazing authors in my journey, and I am excited to be joining with a few of them to bring you The Blushing Brides Christian Romance Series.

This book is dedicated to my amazing Beta readers, especially Shari, who through tough critique made the book better than I imagined.

As always, there's a bit of me in this book. There's even more in the free bonus I'm offering just for signing up for my newsletter.

I hope you love this story of Justin and Ava. If you do, please leave a review at your retailer. It really does make a difference because it lets people make an informed decision about books.

Sign up for Lorana Hoopes's newsletter and get her book, Ava's Blessing in Disguise (listed as Ava's Challenge above until I get a new cover), as a welcome gift. Get Started Now!

The other books in the Blushing Bride series:

The Cowboy's Reality Bride

The Reality Bride's Baby

The Producer's Unlikely Bride

The Cop's Fiery Bride

The Soldier's Stalwart Bride

CHAPTER 1

*J*ustin ran his fingers through his platinum blond hair as he regarded his appearance in the mirror. Every hair belonged in a specific place, and it was integral that all of his lay in their right place. He wasn't looking for a woman - that ship had sailed a long time ago - but one day he hoped to get noticed and offered a better gig than this.

Producing and hosting 'Who Wants to Marry a Cowboy' paid well, but dealing with the happy couples wore on him. It hadn't been so bad when few of the couples lasted, but watching Tyler and Laney find love on the last episode reminded him of his own failed... No, he wouldn't walk down that road again. The past needed to stay there. Locked firmly behind a heavy door with at least three deadbolts and a large wooden beam - just for good measure.

Satisfied that he looked as good as possible, Justin

sprayed a liberal coating of hair spray across his hair. It was the last show of the Maui edition, and the salty ocean breeze always ruffled his hair. He'd cringed when he'd viewed the last episode as his hair had been all over the place. At least the rumors his luxurious hair was a toupee could be put to rest, but tonight, he wanted it to stay in place. One more spray wouldn't hurt. Just for good measure. He gave his hair another coat, winked at his reflection, and then headed for the door.

Carl, the current Cowboy bachelor, would no doubt be waiting nervously at his bungalow. Justin wished they had never chosen him. Calling him indecisive was putting it mildly. Every time a ceremony arose, the man practically broke out in hives and spent half an hour waffling over one girl or the other. The worst part was Justin had to pretend to care. It didn't really matter who Carl picked. Once reality hit and the couples left the show, most didn't make it longer than six months. Tyler and Laney modeled the exception - not the rule.

He knocked on Carl's bungalow, not surprised when the door opened and Carl, a sweaty mess, greeted him by grabbing his hand and yanking him into the room. He clung to Justin's hand as if it were a life vest in the ocean. Cold, clammy sweat seeped into Justin's palm, and he bit his lip to keep from yelling at the man.

"Justin, I'm so glad you're here. I don't know if I can go through with this. Cara and Destiny are both great. I think I love them both. How am I supposed to choose?"

His wild eyes fixed on Justin's. Desperation and urgency swam in them creating a cloudy hue in his gaze.

With as much tact as he could muster, Justin eased his hand from Carl's grip. The clawing need to run it down his pants to wipe off the sheen filled him, but he would not do it. He could feign empathy for a little longer. "You'll do it the way you've done it the whole show, Carl. You'll go with your gut. Choose the one you have the best connection with."

"But what if I'm wrong? What if I choose the wrong woman? I mean this is marriage we're talking about." Carl ran his hand across his chin as he paced the floor.

Justin tried not to roll his eyes. He heard the same story over and over again. Every bachelor except Tyler and Kurt, the other one who married his contestant, said almost the exact same thing. They all believed their choice would affect the rest of their life, but it really only affected their next four to six months. Normally, Justin would say nothing, but today his mouth refused to stay shut. "No one lasts on this show, man. It doesn't matter who you choose."

Carl's mouth opened and closed like a fish trying to get off a hook. He stopped his pacing and ran a hand through his hair. "Are you saying this won't last? No matter what?"

Justin shrugged. He shouldn't have said that. Peter would ream him for saying it, but he was tired. He wanted to sleep, and the truth remained that nearly no one did. "People have, but not many."

Carl crossed the room to stand in front of Justin. His eyes gleamed with intensity. "What did they have? What made them different?" His words clung to Justin like a lost child, but at least his hands stayed by his side.

Therein lay the million-dollar question. If Justin knew what kept couples together, he could help Peter find similar prospects in the future. If matches made on the show actually stayed together, it might skyrocket their viewing. Although Justin wasn't sure whether that was a good thing or not. On one hand, it might get him the exposure he wanted and a hosting role on a more popular show, but on the other, if the show grew too popular, he might not be able to leave.

None of that mattered to Carl who still stared at him with those dopey, hopeful eyes, but he held no words of wisdom for the cowboy. Didn't he know divorce rates reached nearly sixty percent? It didn't matter if you met on a reality dating show or church, the numbers stayed almost the same.

Church. Huh. Justin hadn't realized it at the time, but thinking back now, he was almost certain the other couple who lasted possessed a similar belief in God to Tyler and Laney. Surely that was coincidental though. His parents had been regular church attenders and they still divorced. In fact, his father was on his third or fourth wife by now.

Justin shook his head to clear the wandering thoughts. He clapped a hand on Carl's arm and flashed his pep-talk smile - the one that usually eased contestant's fears and allowed them to breathe easier. "They trusted their heart and didn't let fame go to their heads."

"Fame.... right." Carl said the words slowly and

nodded as he spoke as if seriously considering the words, but Justin knew the idea of fame held his attention more than the letting it go to his head part. Carl was certainly no Tyler. It was obvious from the first meeting that he came on the show to get noticed. He'd shown up with an extra tall hat and a thick southern drawl that wavered in its consistency - thicker when the women were around and barely noticeable with just the two of them. In addition, he flashed a wink at every woman in the room. He'd locked lips with at least three of them the first night, and unlike Tyler, he had made use of the overnight dates. For a man who seemed so worried now, he had certainly appeared flippant throughout the process.

Justin glanced down at his watch. Carl had stalled long enough. "It's time. You ready?"

❧

*A*va McDermott believed in love. She should. It was her job. But she didn't believe in just any kind of love. She believed in the heart thumping, toe tingling, weak in the knees, fireworks bursting, always on my mind kind of love. Which was probably why she remained single. No man seemed to be able to live up to her expectation of love, and she refused to settle for less which led to a lot of frustration.

Normally, she channeled that frustration into her words. She spun characters she would want to date and wove plots that sounded interesting to her and worked, but today.... She had nothing. Ava bit her lip as she stared at her blank screen. The words not only refused to come today, but they taunted her with their refusal to form and stay solid. Every time she thought she had grasped an inkling of the plot the idea would slip away. Her bangs ruffled as she blew out another frustrated breath.

"Everything okay over there?" Genevieve asked from across the room. Gen had been her editor for the last year and her friend for longer. Fantastic at her job, she edited for many authors. She was also vicious. Generally, she tore Ava's books apart, but they always ended up better because of it. Six months ago, they had decided to lease a little office space together.

Ava tapped her fingers lightly on the keyboard in hopes the muscle memory would stir her brain. "I'm having trouble getting words today. Everything feels bland, trite, *passé*."

"How very redundant of you to say the same thing with three different words," Genevieve said with a wry smile. "You know what your problem is, don't you?"

Ava pulled her attention from the inane blinking cursor and focused on her editor. "No, what's my problem?"

"You're running out of experience. When was the last time you went out with a man more than twice?" Gen's eyebrows arched on her forehead and she placed her chin on her folded hands as she posed the question.

"I date," Ava protested. Her last date had been... she thought back and frowned. Okay, it had been awhile.

"Uh huh, but I didn't ask you when your last date was,

though from your face it's been too long. I asked you when was the last time you went out with a man more than twice."

Ava sat straighter in her chair and puffed out her chest. Maybe if she didn't look defeated, Genevieve wouldn't swoop in for the kill. "It's been some time, but none of them have been right."

"You mean none of them have been perfect. You've got this mixed up notion in your head that romance is always fireworks and passion, and that's just not reality."

"But it should be." Ava didn't want the sad relationships that some of her friends had. They fell into two categories: the no longer in love lilies and the flitting fireflies. The no longer in love lilies were her more religious friends - married but bored or unhappy. They claimed fireworks existed once but had faded with time or kids. Now they couldn't remember the last time they held hands or kissed. A few of them even believed they married the wrong person, but their desire to be faithful to God kept them from leaving their spouse.

Then there were the flitting fireflies - friends who jumped into relationships and stayed until the sparks disappeared. Then they left to find a new spark. It didn't matter if they were just dating or married for ten years. They held the mindset that they deserved to be happy, and if their relationship no longer made them happy then it was time to leave.

Ava didn't want to fall into either of those categories. She wanted what her parents had. After forty years of marriage, they remained very much in love. Her father still kissed her mother every day and held her hand as they walked. And if her parents could find it, then she could too. She might just have to kiss a lot more frogs to find her prince.

"Maybe it should be," Genevieve continued, "but it isn't, and if you don't get some new experiences soon, your writing is going to become stale, trite, and *passé*."

Ava stuck out her tongue at Gen, but Gen was right. Almost always right, Gen doled out sage advice, but that didn't mean Ava could just wave a wand and find a man she wanted to date.

"Look," Genevieve stood and crossed the space between them, "maybe you need a break. Why don't you go somewhere different for a week and see if it opens up your creative juices?"

A week. Could she afford to be gone a week? Ava enjoyed writing. It was certainly more rewarding than her previous job selling insurance had been, but the one thing that irked her was the ebb and flow. She had saved six months' salary before quitting her day job, and two months ago she had sold a plethora of books and enjoyed a spike in her income. However, last month she hadn't released anything. Now, she was watching her income drop, and it was stressful to say the least. She needed to finish this book and release it because even though the words weren't coming, she still had a mortgage payment and a car payment due. They weren't going to care that the words refused to come as easily this time. She couldn't call them and use writer's block as an excuse for why she couldn't pay her bills. Well, she could, but she doubted they would have any sympathy for her.

"Yeah, maybe." Ava closed her eyes. Maybe closed, she could see the picture unfold. That's how the last book had been. She'd prayed for words, shut her eyes, and seen a movie in her head. Then she'd written until the words ran dry. The next night had been the same and every night after until the book was done.

Maybe the difference resided there. She hadn't taken this book directly to God in prayer when she started. She'd run with an idea in her head that matched the flow in the market, but while the first thousand words had poured out, now she was stuck.

She waited. For an idea, a feeling, a word, but the only image that kept popping into her head was the ocean. The gently lapping waves, the smell of salt, the soft caress of the wind on her skin. How long had it been since she had visited the ocean? Too long for sure, but she remembered always feeling inspired when there. Was that what she was supposed to do? Go to the ocean?

Ava gave it another few minutes, but only the picture of the ocean remained. She opened her eyes. "All I see is the ocean, so I guess the ocean it is." With a shrug, she clicked a new browser open and began searching rental houses near the ocean. A hotel or an inn wouldn't work. She needed a quiet space that would have little interruption from others.

"The ocean is good," Genevieve said as she came behind Ava and watched over her shoulder.

A quaint white cottage appeared on the screen. From the picture it appeared the cottage sat right on the beach as the expansive blue could be seen to the left. Two palm trees that held a hammock between them sat on the right, and the sand appeared to glisten in the picture.

Ava grinned up at Genevieve. "And this might be perfect."

"It sure looks pretty although a little lonely. Not sure where you'll meet a man around there."

"I'm not going to meet a man," Ava said, "I'm *going* to get inspired."

Genevieve held up a hand in surrender before returning to her desk.

Ava turned back to the screen and scanned the information. The rate appeared reasonable and it appeared the cottage came with a kitchen to prepare your own meals, a utility room with a washer and dryer, and wi-fi. Even better. She could totally unplug and still get work done. At the bottom of the page was the rental company's information. Reflection Rentals. Sounded interesting. Ava picked up her cell phone and punched in the number.

"Reflection Rentals, how may I help you?" The warm voice on the other end reminded Ava of her grandmother, and the smell of the chocolate chip cookies her grandmother always baked filled her memory.

"Hello, I'm interested in renting your cottage on the beach." Ava scrolled back up searching for a name, but there wasn't one. "It has no name, but it's the quaint white one."

"Ah, that's our slice of tranquility," the woman said.

"Is that what it's called?" Ava asked.

A gentle laugh filled her ear. "No, dear, it doesn't have an official name, but that's what I like to call it."

"I see. Well, is it available to rent?" She would need a few days to pack and make sure she had someone to check on her place. "I could be there Sunday, and I'd like to have it for at least a week."

"Of course. I can certainly do that for you. What's your name, dear?"

"Ava McDermott." Ava rattled off the rest of her information including her credit card and then hung up. She still had no words, but she had a plan, and hopefully the words would come when she followed the plan.

CHAPTER 2

*J*ustin sighed in relief as the last light flicked off. This Maui show had felt so much longer than the others. Was it because exhaustion covered him? Irritation he hadn't gotten to do much sightseeing? Or something more? Could it be that watching all this love and facing his loveless life was wearing thin on him? He relaxed into the approaching darkness.

"Justin, I need a word."

And the relaxation flew out the window. The tone in Peter's voice sent chills down Justin's back, and he hurriedly searched his memory for any reason Peter might be upset with him. He hadn't sent out any new auditions yet, so the likelihood he knew about those was small. Besides, Peter had to know this wasn't a permanent gig for Justin. Justin had told him that at the beginning when they'd partnered as producers. True that had been a decade ago, but still…

"Sure, Peter, what's up?" Justin glanced around for something to do to keep from focusing on Peter. He knew from experience that when Peter's voice took on the deep timbre that nothing good was coming next. The only problem was that there was nothing around. The crew had packed up and vanished like ghosts, almost as if they knew this discussion would be happening. There was nothing around them but sand.

"I want you to take some time off," Peter began.

Justin sagged with relief. Time off? He'd planned to take some anyway. Now, he had his partner's blessing. Even better. "Of course Peter, now that this show has wrapped-"

"I wasn't finished." It wasn't quite anger, but there was a definite forcefulness to Peter's voice that shut Justin up and sent the dread coursing through him once again. "It is obvious from your behavior of late that you need some time away from the show."

"My behavior?" Justin swallowed the words quickly afraid his tone would invoke suspicion.

Peter shot him one of those 'you know what I'm talking about stares.' The kind that could make you feel guilty even if you had done nothing wrong, but Justin knew he was off his game. He had just hoped no one else had noticed it. "Yes, your behavior. Bringing the reporters to Tyler's and Laney's wedding hoping to break them up-"

Justin held up a hand and shook his head. "In my defense, those two were over the top sweet and besides it didn't work."

Peter continued as if Justin hadn't interrupted him,

"Setting up all these physical dates to make the women look bad."

"Carl said he wanted an active woman." It wasn't why Justin had planned the dates he had, but it was a good excuse.

"And telling Carl it didn't matter who he chose?"

Justin cringed at that one. He shouldn't have done that. Technically, he had broken contract and Peter could fire him for that. "That was a mistake, but if you had heard him and his indecision-"

Peter rolled his eyes and the volume of his voice rose in exasperation. "He was undecided because he was making a huge decision. Our goal is to find these men and women love, remember?"

Justin remembered. He just couldn't seem to make himself care. When they'd started this show, he had been young and in love, but then tragedy had struck and love had turned its back on him. Now, the idea of a happily ever after left him feeling empty and jaded.

Peter took a deep breath, composing himself. His next words came out softer. "So, I think you need to go get your head on straight. Take some time and remember why we are doing this job."

"Fine. I'll take some time. I'll go visit my sister or something." His sister lived in Washington state with her husband, two point five kids, and the perfect job, so the thought of visiting her held little appeal, but at least it would get Peter off his back.

"No, I've already booked the place you are going. I'm sending you to the slice of tranquility."

"The what?" Even the name sounded awful to Justin. He didn't need tranquility. Well, maybe he did, but he didn't need to go to a place named that. It would probably be adorned with fuzzy bathrobes and yoga meetings and green smoothies made with algae instead of coffee.

"The slice of tranquility. That's what Margie called it anyway. It's the cabin where I met my wife."

"You met your wife at a cabin?" Justin was thoroughly confused. Was he supposed to be at this cabin to relax or find love?

Peter waved a hand. "It's a long story. Anyway, I've booked it for you. It's right on the ocean. You can relax," his eyes wandered to Justin's hair, "let your hair down a little, and come back refreshed."

"In case you haven't noticed, Peter, we're at the beach." He gestured widely at the surrounding sand. "We've been in Hawaii for the last few months."

"Yes, but you've been working, not relaxing. Besides magical things happen at this cabin." The corners of Peter's lips twitched and his eyes took on a faraway look as if he was remembering some magical thing that had taken place.

"Fine." Justin didn't think a cabin at the beach would solve his problems, but he definitely wanted to wipe that expression off Peter's face. Besides, he could use some time away to figure out if he wanted to stay with the show or pursue other options full time. "Just give me the information."

~

*A*va pulled into the Reflections Rental office and turned off the car. Even this building exuded a sense of peace and tranquility. Nestled into a grove of trees, it blended in with the white sand around it. No other cars sat around the building, and Ava wondered where the employees parked.

The quiet pressed in on her as she approached the building. There was no traffic, no hum of conversation, not even the chirping of birds. It was as if time stood still here, in its own little bubble.

A tiny bell jingled as she pushed open the door. The sound reminded Ava of the fairy wings effect in a show she used to love as a child. Every time a fairy received wings or used them in some magical way, there would be this tinkling sound. Ava remembered nothing else from the show - not the name of it or the story lines, but that sound somehow imprinted on her mind.

The door shut softly behind her and a soft warm scent of vanilla floated through the air adding to the homey feel. Once again, Ava felt transported back to her grandmother's house where it always smelled of cookies and love. A woman with hair that resembled fluffy white marshmallows looked up from the lone desk as Ava entered.

"Oh, hello, dear, you must be Ava. I'm Margie." Her smile lit up the room and her warm demeanor put Ava immediately at ease. Though impeded by her age and a slight limp in her right leg, Margie ambled toward Ava, her weathered hand outstretched. Ava felt as if she were in a dream. Margie reminded her of someone - and not just that grandmother feel - but there was something more.

"I am." Ava shook the hand not realizing she had even lifted her own.

Margie's other hand closed over their clasped hands, and Ava felt frozen, as if glue held her feet in place. Warmth flooded her along with a feeling of safety, but that was silly. She didn't even know this woman. "I just know you will have a fantastic time. Let me get you the keys."

She dropped their hands, and Ava blinked. The warmth receded from her body though it still circled through the room just out of touch. She followed Margie back to the desk where a stack of papers sat prominently in the middle. Margie rifled through the papers, shaking her head and emitting soft murmurs as she turned the pages. "Ah, here we go. I just need you to sign here." She handed the paper and a pen to Ava.

Ava scanned the contract, but nothing seemed out of the ordinary. She was responsible for her own meals and her laundry, but she knew that going in. The cottage also needed to be in the same condition when she left - again, understandable. Only one clause seemed odd. If perhaps the cottage was double booked, she agreed to give it three days before asking for a refund.

"Does this happen often?" she asked pointing at the odd clause.

Margie looked down and then waved her hand. "Oh, hardly ever, but it did happen one time, and it makes more sense to have the information there. You know what I mean?"

"Right, so does this mean if it gets double booked that I have to stay there with someone else for three days to qualify for the refund?"

Margie's white hair bounced with her nod. "It does, but again, it hardly ever happens. I'm sure you have nothing to worry about."

Ava nodded but in the back of her mind she thought it would be just her luck if it happened to her. Especially when she really needed the quiet. Still, she was here and it was paid for. She signed her name to the bottom and handed the contract back.

"Wonderful. Here's the key and the map to get there. It's a little off the beaten path, so make sure you watch for the signs."

The words triggered something in Ava's head. A memory? A feeling? She wasn't sure. "What did you say?"

"I said watch for the signs, dearie." She placed the key and map in Ava's hand. "They're there to guide you."

"Right. Thank you." Those seemed odd words for Margie to say, but the woman was older. Maybe it was her way.

The map proved a little challenging to follow, and twice Ava almost missed the turn. Only the small wooden signs that read simply Tranquility with an arrow saved her, but the view was worth the challenge when she arrived. The ocean spread, a blue blanket, for as far as she could see. Was this a private beach?

Warm, salty air caressed her skin as she stepped out of the car. A light breeze ruffled her dark hair, and the sun rained soft kisses on her face. This she could get used to. Fear and worry rolled off her shoulders as she stepped into the cabin which was larger than it had looked in the picture.

The immediate room welcomed her with a charming fireplace and large plush furniture. Her favorite was a cushy chair in the corner by the window. A lamp nestled behind it as if protecting it with its glow, and the chair faced the window which looked out at the expansive ocean. It would be the perfect place for her to work. She could almost feel the creative energy flowing through her as she pictured sitting there.

A hallway led out of the room and opened to the kitchen patterned with cottages and beach prints. It wasn't large, and the only seating was a small table with two chairs, but Ava didn't figure she would spend much time in here anyway. Long enough to prepare the food, but she'd much rather eat it facing the window or better yet outside. A sliding glass door lay behind the table and it led right out to the beach. Ava could see a small table and two chairs outside. Perhaps that was where she would eat.

She checked the cupboards, but they were empty as was the refrigerator. No matter, Ava had brought food with her. Beyond the kitchen were two bedrooms each about the same size and color pallet. They both contained a private bathroom which seemed a little odd in a two bedroom, but Ava certainly didn't mind. She disliked hotels that had no bathroom in the room and forced her to walk down the hall, often in the dark early morning hours.

She deposited her suitcase on the bed of one of the rooms - the one with the view of the hammock as the other just had a view of the beach but no ocean - and then returned to the car for the cooler of food she had brought. It should be enough to last her a week, and then she figured she would either be finished with her book or she could take a break and drive to the nearest town for more.

With the food unpacked and put away, Ava grabbed her notebook and headed outside. She couldn't wait to feel the sand between her toes and soak up the inspiration from the waves. Surely, here she would find inspiration. How could she not?

CHAPTER 3

J ustin pulled up to the rental office and sighed.
The place appeared bland and tiny. He had
no idea why Peter had gone with this place -
maybe it had once looked better - but what choice did he
have? At least it was paid for.

One of those annoying bells jingled announcing his
arrival as he opened the door. An elderly woman, probably
in her seventies looked up at him. "Welcome, dearie, I'll be
right with you."

Oh great. Not only was the place miniscule but one
little old lady ran it. What would the cabin look like?
Probably run down and in need of repairs. He doubted a
woman her age could keep up with landlord demands.
Justin rolled his eyes. This place might have been great
years ago when Peter met his wife, but Justin doubted it
would look the same now.

"All right, dear, sorry about that. Come have a seat and tell me how I can help you."

"My name is Justin Miller. I believe my boss, Peter, rented me a cabin for the week."

The woman looked up in surprise. "Miller? You're English then?"

What an odd question. What did his background have to do with renting a cabin? "Uh, yeah, I guess. Does that matter?"

She tilted her head up and glanced up at the ceiling. Justin followed her gaze but saw nothing there. Great, she was crazy too.

"No, I suppose it doesn't," she said after a minute. "He's up for the challenge."

"He?" Justin glanced around the room just to make sure he hadn't missed anything, but the second glance revealed the same thing the first had - a tiny room with no hidden doors.

"My boss," she stated as if that explained it all. "Here's your contract, dearie. Sign at the bottom and I can get you the key."

"Right." Justin didn't bother to read the contract. Peter was paying for it anyway. He finished his signature with a flourish and handed the paper back to the elderly woman.

She scanned it and flashed a large smile. "Here's your key and a map to the cottage."

"I doubt I need a map."

"It's a little tricky to get there, so take it just in case and be sure and watch for the signs."

"I think I can handle it," Justin said as he took the key and the map from her.

He shook his head as he left the rental office and walked back to his car. That had been an odd experience to say the least. He climbed inside and tossed the key and the map on the passenger seat. Justin doubted he would need the map, but the woman - he hadn't even gotten her name - had been rather insistent that he took it.

As he started the car, Justin hoped the rest of his trip would be less weird. If it wasn't, Peter definitely owed him.

Half an hour and three missed turns later, Justin pulled up in front of the cottage surprised to see another car parked there. Perhaps it was the cleaning crew or something. He couldn't imagine anyone would find this place by accident.

He shook his head as he stepped out of the car. Someone should tell that woman at the rental office to make those signs larger as he'd missed every one of them the first time. Of course he probably could have been paying closer attention, but that was beside the point. He grabbed his bag from the trunk and slugged his way to the front door. Suitcases with wheels and sandy beaches went together about as well as peanut butter and catfish.

At least the view was nice. The cabin itself wasn't much to look at, but the expansive ocean to the left of it took his breath away. Justin felt the tension easing off his shoulders with each gentle lap of the waves on the beach just feet away. And to the right, a hammock swung lazily back and forth in the breeze. He would definitely be spending some quality time there.

He turned the handle expecting to find it locked, but the front door swung open. That seemed rather trusting of the rental company; weren't they afraid someone would come in and steal things? But the place was secluded. Maybe they left it unlocked because no one would ever find it without a map or perhaps the cleaning crew left it unlocked while they cleaned. Justin shut the door behind him and took in the room. Or maybe it was unlocked because there was nothing here to steal, he thought with a sigh.

The simple room bordered on being drab. Nothing sat atop the fireplace mantle, only a few pieces of artwork hung around the room, and even the bookshelf held slim pickings. Worn furniture completed the room. Yep, that hammock was looking better by the minute.

Justin left his suitcase by the door and continued farther in. A kitchen appeared on his left. Nothing fancy, but useable. He opened a cabinet door, surprised to find food inside. Peter hadn't told him he needed to bring his own food, but he'd brought a few things just in case. It was nice of the company to stock food, but he wondered if this was for him or left from the previous guest.

A glance in the fridge revealed fresh milk and a case of Code Red Mountain Dew - his favorite drink. He had no idea how they knew about that, but he didn't care. A cold beverage sounded perfect right now. He swiped one from the cardboard box, popped the lid, and took a satisfying swig before continuing down the hallway.

There were only two more doors which meant either two bedrooms or perhaps one bedroom and a bathroom though he rather hoped it was the former. It wouldn't really matter since he was the only one here, but he hated having to leave the comfort of his bedroom to use the bathroom.

As he pushed open the door of the first room, the sound of running water carried out. The cleaning crew must be working in the bathroom. He stepped inside, and the sound stopped. Had he imagined it? A floorboard creaked. No, someone was definitely in the bathroom. His eyes darted around the room for something he could use as a weapon in case it wasn't the cleaning staff, but there was nothing. The room was sparsely furnished, just a bed and a dresser, but what his eyes did land on was the suitcase.

It was definitely not his suitcase. He'd left his by the door, and it was black, not the bright purple color staring back at him. So, then whose suitcase was it?

The feminine scream gave him only a second to respond before a crazed wet creature in a towel flew at him.

~

*A*va's shrill scream echoed in her ears as she lunged across the room at the intruder. Who was he? And how had he gotten in? She had no idea how she managed to keep her towel on as her hands curled into fists and rained down on the man. The drink in his hand - her Mountain Dew - went flying as he defended himself.

He grabbed her hands and quickly pinned her wrists stopping her punches. "Who are you? And what are you doing in my cottage?" His gruff voice matched the strength in his hands.

"Your cottage?" She struggled to get her hands free, but his grip held firm. "This is my cottage. At least for the next week. Now, will you let go of me?"

"Do you promise to stop hitting me?"

"Stop hitting you? You're a strange man in my bedroom. I think I have every right to defend myself." But even as she said the words, her fear lessened. He didn't seem dangerous. Stiff perhaps if his hair was any indication, but he'd made no move to attack her, and he was clearly stronger than she was. Struggling would only wear her out.

"There's obviously been a mistake and we can figure it out, but only if you calm down."

Ava nodded but kept her guard up as he dropped her hands. "Okay, I'm calm, but you're still in the wrong cottage. I have a rental agreement that says I have this place."

The man held up his hand in a surrendering posture. "So do I. Look, why don't you get dressed and then come out to the kitchen. We can figure out what happened then."

Ava narrowed her eyes at him. "Fine, but don't touch

my stuff." She eyed the can that was slowly pouring liquid on the floor. "Or any more of my food."

He followed her gaze and then bent down and picked up the can. "I'll find a towel to clean the floor."

"Don't bother," she said. "I'll use this one after I'm dressed."

His eyes dropped to her towel and Ava's face grew hot. Way to pull attention to the fact that only a small piece of cloth was keeping her covered. "Right." He cleared his throat. "I'll just be-" He pointed awkwardly at the door before turning and darting out to the hallway.

With the door shut and locked, Ava quickly finished drying and dressed. Even though the weather was warm, she tugged on her most modest shirt and shorts. She didn't think he was dangerous, but there was no need to go tempting fate either. She dropped the towel on the red puddle and wiped it up then deposited the towel in the laundry hamper on her way out the door.

As she neared the kitchen, she pulled back her shoulders putting on a brave exterior. She was a strong, independent, assertive woman, and he was clearly in the wrong place. He sat at the small table, his phone in his hand, but he stood when she entered.

"Tea?" she asked before he could say anything. The situation was uncomfortable as it was, but sitting across from the stranger with nothing to occupy her hands sounded like torture.

"Do you have any coffee?"

"There's a pot." She pointed to the contraption on the

counter. "But I don't drink the stuff and I didn't bring any."

"Tea is fine," he conceded and sat back down.

Ava filled the kettle in the sink and then turned the burner on before rummaging in the cabinets. She brought down two mugs and pulled out two tea bags from the stash she had brought placing one in each mug. She was thankful that she had something to keep her hands occupied and a reason not to be looking at him.

When the kettle whistled, she finally turned to him. "Do you take anything in it?"

"Cream and sugar, I guess," he answered. "I'm not really much of a tea guy."

Ava nodded, unsurprised by this declaration, and opened the fridge. She retrieved the cream and set it on the table next to the sugar. Then she grabbed the mugs. "So, what are we going to do about this?" She kept her tone even though her hands shook slightly as she lifted her mug.

"I suppose we should check the rental agreements and find out which one of us in the wrong place."

Ava did not miss the condescension in his voice. He obviously had money or wanted people to believe he did. His manicured hands, perfectly coiffed hair, and designer shirt did not go unnoticed. "Uh huh, well I have mine and I can assure you that I'm in the right place. I followed Margie's map to a T."

He pushed his chair back. "I have mine as well. I'll just grab it and we can put this to rest." He strode out of the room with a purposeful gait and returned a moment later with a single sheet of paper in hand. With an exaggerated flourish, he placed the paper on the table in front of her.

She picked it up expecting to find something wrong - the date, the name of the cottage, something - but there was nothing off. His paper looked exactly like hers. "But I don't... oh no." She shook her head in disbelief. What were the odds?

"Oh no, what?" he asked as he sat again.

Ava sighed and ran a hand across the bridge of her nose. "Did you read the contract?"

The man shrugged. "I skimmed it."

"Of course you did." A judgmental edge filled her voice, but she didn't care. "There's a clause in the agreement about what happens if they double book the cottage. I asked about it because I thought it was odd, but Margie assured me it rarely happens."

"Wait, there's a clause about this? What does it say?"

Ava rolled her eyes. Why did people sign things they didn't read? "That we have to give it at least three days before asking for a refund."

"What?" His eyes widened making the ocean blue color of them even more prominent. "That's preposterous. They overbooked and they make us wait three days for a refund? I don't think so. We should go have a talk with that woman."

"Margie. Her name is Margie."

"I don't care what her name is." His hands splayed across the table, large and tan.

Ava wondered if the color was natural or from a bottle.

She could never tan. Her father's Scottish genes ran too strong in her pale skin, but every time she tried tanner from a bottle, it left her orange and streaky. She'd given up years ago.

"I'm not sharing the space for three days with a crazy woman I don't even know. No offense." He added the last two words quickly as if they could erase the harsh words he had spewed at her just before them.

Ava prickled and leaned back in her chair crossing her arms. Whether it was conscious or not, she enjoyed the added distance the movement brought. She generally prided herself on keeping a cool head, but this man managed to hit all her buttons. "First of all, I am not crazy. You were in my bedroom. I had every right to attack you, and this is not my idea of fun either. I came here to work, and I need peace and quiet."

They locked gazes almost as if engaging in an unspoken game of chicken. Whoever spoke first would show their weakness, and Ava had decided it wasn't going to be her. She didn't know who this perfect, plastic man was, but she wasn't about to let him steamroll her.

"Fine," he said finally. "Get your agreement and let's go see if anything can be done."

CHAPTER 4

*J*ustin shook his head as he watched the raven-haired woman rise and walk away from the table. She was a spit-fire for sure and nice to look at, but that didn't mean he wanted to share his space with her. He had come here to get away from couples and love, and the last thing he needed was to be thrown into this small space with a woman. A very attractive, aggravating woman.

"Okay, here it is, and it's exactly what I said." She waved a piece of paper at him.

He stood. "Can I see it?" There was no use making a trip just to get there and find out this woman had been mistaken.

She cocked a raised brow at him, her expression a challenge. "You don't believe me?"

Justin shrugged. He didn't trust a lot of people, and women usually graced the top of the list of people he didn't trust. "I don't even know you, but I've proven my contract was right. It's only fair you show me yours."

Her lips pursed together though the corners twitched. Her blue eyes twinkled at him. "I assume you're still talking about my contract."

He replayed his words in his head smirking a little when he realized what he'd said. So, she had a sense of humor. That was refreshing as his ex-wife hadn't seemed to. Well, unless you considered her leaving him for her Botox doctor a sense of humor. Still, he wondered if this stranger could take what she dished out. "I was unless you had another suggestion."

Her posture stiffened, and her smile faded as a light pink color floated across her face. "No. I most certainly did not. Here."

She thrust the paper at him as if his words had lit it on fire. He scanned it, but her contract appeared as valid as his.

"Satisfied?" Her rigid demeanor had returned, the humor gone.

"Not really. I was hoping to unwind, but instead I have to get this fixed with a woman I don't know." He stepped toward the front door.

"Ava."

"What?" He turned back to her.

"My *name* is Ava. If we're stuck together, we might as well use names."

He couldn't care less about her name. His hope was the rental company would figure this out and relocate one of them, even if it was him. He didn't care what cottage he stayed in as long as he was the only one in it. "Justin," he said, but he didn't offer his hand. "Can we go now?"

"By all means. Lead the way." Sarcasm flowed out of her voice, but Justin didn't take the bait. He simply wanted to get this cleared up and get away from her.

He headed toward his car, but the woman stepped toward the other car as they exited the cottage. "Where are you going? I'm parked right here."

She crossed her arms. "I don't know you. I'm not getting in a car with you when you might be some serial killer or something."

"I'm not a…" Justin sighed and shook his head in frustration. "I'm not a serial killer. I'm a producer and the host of Who Wants to Marry a Cowboy."

She blinked at him, her expression deadpan. "Is that supposed to mean something to me?"

This. This reaction was exactly why he needed a new job. He didn't even care if it was just producing though he preferred being in front of the cameras, but he needed something that people knew. Some job that would allow him to be recognized. "It's a reality dating show. We've been around for ten years."

Ava shrugged. "I don't watch much television. I'm a writer, so I'm more focused on my own stories."

A writer? That piqued his interest slightly. He wondered what she wrote but only briefly. Unless she was a screenwriter who worked for a large studio and could get him an acting job, he doubted they would have much in common. Though he thought it silly, if she wanted to drive herself, he wasn't going to stop her. "Suit yourself. I'll see you there."

~

*A*va shook her head as she climbed into her own car. Not only was he a distraction, but Justin was a piece of work. Why wasn't he staying at some fancy schmancy hotel instead of at this little cottage? Maybe his money was all a facade. He seemed like the type to want to have prestige and therefore pretended he did in hopes of fooling people.

She shook her head as she opened her door. She didn't know him, so she shouldn't be judging him, but he certainly made it hard not to.

He was already parked at the rental office when she arrived, but he hadn't gone in yet. He opened his car door as she did. Was he afraid of little old Margie? Or was it just that he hoped a unified front might help their case?

Ava pulled on the door handle but it didn't budge. It was locked in the middle of the day?

"What's the problem?" Justin asked coming up beside her.

"It's locked." She cupped her hands around her face and leaned closer but she could see no movement inside.

"What? That's not possible. I just came from here fifteen minutes ago." As if he thought the problem was just her strength, he pulled on the door handle himself.

"Maybe you were the last client for the day."

"At just past noon? That makes no sense." He pulled again on the handle and then began banging on the glass.

Of course he thought brute strength was the answer. "Maybe she took a break. Regardless, no one is in there. Let's just go back and call. We can leave a message to have her return the call when she gets back in."

"And then what? I came for peace and quiet."

Ava's fuse burned again. Did he know how obnoxious he was or was that just his character flaw? She flashed a tight-lipped smile at him as she bit her words out. "Well lucky for you, I need quiet to write as well. We can figure out a schedule for the main room and avoid each other as much as possible until this gets fixed."

He stared at her for a moment before rolling his eyes and sighing. "Fine. I guess we don't have much choice."

At that moment, Margie appeared from the side of the building. "Ava, so good to see you again. Oh, and Justin too. I hope you weren't waiting long." She inserted the key and pulled open the front door seemingly oblivious to their stiff postures. "Come in, come in. To what do I owe this pleasure?"

"Pleasure? You double booked us." Justin's angry voice carried over her shoulder as they stepped into the office and Ava silenced him with a pointed stare.

She tried for a calmer tone. "Justin's right, Margie. Evidently, we both got approved for the cottage this week, and uh that doesn't really work for us. I need quiet to work, and he…"

"I need my own space," he finished for her.

Margie's face wrinkled in concern. "Oh dear, I'm so sorry that happened. Can I see your contracts?"

Ava and Justin handed their papers over and Margie scanned them. "It does appear we made a mistake. My assistant must have booked this one without me knowing."

Ava glanced around, but she saw no other desk nor a place for one.

"We don't care who made the mistake," Justin said stepping forward. "We just want it fixed. Surely, you have another cottage one of us could take instead."

"I'm afraid not," Margie said. "We're booked solid."

"But... we can't both stay there," Ava said. "It wouldn't be proper."

"I'm sure you can work something out," Margie said with a slight smile. "It does have two bedrooms, and while we'll be happy to refund if it doesn't work out, our policy is three days."

"What kind of policy is that?" Justin asked stepping forward.

Ava placed a restraining hand on his arm. "We can figure something out for three days."

He glanced down at her hand, and his voice softened. "Fine. Three days."

"Good luck you two," Margie called as they exited the office. As they climbed in their separate cars, Ava thought they would need a lot more than luck.

Suddenly she wondered if she might have more luck reaching Margie without Justin's abrasive personality filling the room. She opened her car door and headed back toward the front door of the office.

He rolled down his window and shot her an inquisitive look. "What are you doing?"

"Go ahead," she said with a wave. "I'll be right behind you. I just forgot something."

With a curt nod, he rolled up his window and backed out of the parking lot. Ava pulled the door open and stepped inside. "Margie?"

"Did you forget something dearie?"

"I just thought…" she sighed as she tried to form the diplomatic words she wanted to say. "I know Justin can be…. blunt (and that was putting it mildly), but we really can't stay in the same cabin. Surely, there's something you can do."

"Are you a believer Ava?"

"I am which is why I shouldn't stay in the same cottage with him even if it does have two rooms."

Margie nodded. "And do you believe that God makes mistakes?"

"Of course not, but what does that have to do with anything?"

Margie smiled her sweet, grandmotherly smile but said nothing. Was she trying to say God had made sure they were double booked? But why would He do that? It was clear she and Justin were nearly complete opposites. "All right, well, thank you, Margie, and please call if something opens up sooner."

Bewildered by the exchange, Ava left the office for the second time and headed back to the cottage.

Justin was sitting at the table scowling when she entered. "Okay, so how do you propose we make this work?"

She sat across from him and folded her hands together on the table. Sweet, she would be sweet. "Well, my best writing time is in the morning, and while I could write in my room, the view in the main room is more inspiring."

"So, you want me to stay out of the main room the whole morning?" Justin's face morphed into a portrait of contempt.

Nope, sweet flew out the window, and she glared at him. This wasn't how she had planned to spend her time at the cottage either. "No, but if that could be quiet time until lunch. That way I could still get writing done."

He matched her stare for a moment before rolling his eyes. "Fine. I can make that work. I'll go surfing or something."

"You surf?" She couldn't picture him surfing. Even the jeans he wore currently had a pressed line on them. She didn't know anyone ironed jeans. She certainly didn't, but then again she didn't mind wrinkles. In fact, she was probably on a first name basis with wrinkles, but she chalked that up to her hate/hate relationship with irons. *That* had started after an unfortunate burn incident she rarely discussed except when someone noticed the odd scar on her side.

"I used to."

She waited for him to say more, but it appeared he was done sharing. She supposed if she imagined hard enough, he did have a slight surfer air, but like someone who had spent their time that way years ago. Though he appeared to be in shape, it wasn't the lean shape of a surfer, more the muscular shape of a gym rat. Well, at least if he was outside, she might still get some work done. It wasn't how she planned it, but it might be doable IF he kept up his end of the bargain. "All right. As long as you stay out of my food. And my drinks." Justin's eyes fell to the table. "You did bring your own food, didn't you?"

"Yeah, some. My boss booked this cottage for me." He shrugged. "I assumed food would be supplied."

Of course he did. He probably thought they cleaned the place too. Obviously he hadn't read the contract. Ava wondered why his boss had booked the cottage. Was this a reward or a punishment?

"But I can go get more," he continued, "there's a town not too far from here."

"That would be a good idea as I only brought enough for myself. I wasn't planning on feeding Hollywood's elite." Ugh, what was it about him that brought out the worst in her? She wasn't generally so snarky.

Justin chuckled. "I'm certainly no Hollywood elite. So, what do we do? Shake on it?"

"Works for me." Ava stuck out her hand and he took it. She was rather surprised not to feel utter revulsion at his touch since everything else about him bugged her immensely.

"Right, well, I'll get out of your hair and go buy more groceries." He stood and shifted from one foot to the other. Was he nervous? It was the first chink she had seen in his cocky demeanor. "You'll have to free up a shelf for me though." And the chink was gone.

He tossed the comment at her as he walked out the door, so there was no chance for her to respond. Probably a good thing anyway. She doubted her response would have been very Christian. With a shake of her head, she stood and walked to her room to retrieve her laptop.

Once back in the main room, she settled into the comfy chair and opened her laptop. The cursor blinked at her expectantly. How she hated that cursed cursor lately. She placed her fingers on the keys willing the words to come, but still no creativity flowed. Instead all she saw was Justin's perfect hair, his haughty eyes, and his cocky smile. Oh great, now not only was he a distraction, but he was invading her thoughts as well.

But perhaps she could use that to her advantage. Maybe she could write her frustrations with him into her novel. She closed her eyes and took a deep breath. Yes, there was the story, tugging slightly at the back of her mind. She coaxed it forward, promising it grandeur if it would come into the light, and it did.

A small smile graced her lips as her fingers began flying across the keys. Only twice did she look up, once to admire the ocean and once when the door opened and Justin slipped back inside.

*J*ustin listened to the clacking keys of her computer and wondered what she was writing. It must be something interesting because other than the brief glance she gave him when he stepped through the front door with his food, she hadn't stopped. She just kept tapping away.

He opened the freezer and shoved his tv dinners in. Not his normal fare, but the food had been limited at the tiny store and he hadn't cooked for himself in months, so he'd been hesitant to buy a ton of fresh food that he'd probably butcher without a recipe. At least with these, he wouldn't go hungry. He had picked up hamburger meat though. Although he wasn't sure a grill existed at the cottage, he could make a mean hamburger in a skillet if necessary.

Maybe she wasn't writing anything at all. Perhaps it

was all a show and she simply typed random letters to appear busy. That would be some dedication to a ruse though. You could only type nonsense for so long before boredom killed you. Besides, she had looked focused.

Her long dark hair had been pulled back in a loose ponytail, and her eyes caught his with a look of surprise - almost as if she had been so into her writing she hadn't heard him arrive. Was he ever that focused on anything? He supposed he had been that focused on the show once back when he and Peter were just planning it. Back when Carol had been alive and challenging him to be the best he could be.

Justin shook his head as he shut the fridge door and turned to the cupboard. He would not think about Carol or Candy or any of the other women from his past. His job here was to clear his mind of negative thoughts and either refocus on the show or cut his ties once and for all.

The clacking stopped and he froze, his hand extended into the cupboard. Had she stopped? Why? He let go of the can of green beans and checked his watch. It was nearly four, so she must have decided to take a break. He wondered if she would leave her laptop out. Curiosity coursed through his veins. He supposed he could just ask her, but then she would know he was curious, and he didn't need that. She might confuse his curiosity for interest and it certainly wasn't that.

The front door opened and closed. She had gone outside. He finished putting the cans away and stepped back into the main room, his eyes tearing eagerly toward the corner where she had been sitting, but her computer was gone. He hadn't heard her walk past so had she taken it outside then?

Drawn by a force he couldn't name or understand, Justin crossed to the place she had vacated and sat down. A sweet scent of flowers hung in the air. Her perfume? Shampoo? He understood why she chose this spot. The chair not only molded to his frame, but the window looked out on the ocean.

As he watched, she came into view. The breeze lifted strands of her hair blowing them to the side like brushstrokes on a painting. Her face tilted up as if she were soaking up the sun, and then she walked out of view. A part of him wanted to get up from the chair, to press his face to the window and watch where she walked, but he would not do that. Ava might be intriguing, but she was still a woman. And he had terrible luck with women.

~

*A*va returned to the cottage when her watch read six. She enjoyed walking the beach and not thinking for a few hours. There was something refreshing in just letting go, but now her stomach yearned for some food and her fingers itched to add a little more to her story even if she had to do it in the small bedroom.

She opened the cottage door surprised to find Justin

asleep in the cushy chair. He actually looked human and vulnerable passed out with his mouth slightly open. Too bad he was so cocky when he was awake. She wondered what made him that way. Was it working in television? Had he grown up that way?

Ava shook her head as she walked past him to the kitchen. She was dissecting him like he was a character in her book, although she guessed in a way he was though she doubted the past she had given her character matched his past. It might be interesting to find out though. She loved writing about people she knew as it always seemed to bring her characters to life. It was even more fun to write about people she saw and imagine their back stories. It annoyed her friends though and they chastised her whenever they caught her staring at people.

She couldn't help it though as she'd been a people watcher from a very young age. Her mother often dragged her older brother and sister and her along on shopping trips. Whenever they ventured to the mall, her mother would buy them two soft pretzels to share, and they would sit on a bench and observe people as they walked by. Her mother would lean over after someone passed and make up a story for them. "See that guy with a limp? He was teaching his daughter to drive, and she accidentally put the car in reverse and drove over his foot. They raced to the hospital, but while they were waiting to be seen, an old woman who was half blind didn't see him as she passed and she stabbed his foot with her cane. By the time he saw a doctor, he lost all feeling in three of his five toes, and it never came back." And that was how it began.

After that, Ava observed everyone wherever she went. She watched their mannerisms and their clothing choices, committing them to memory. When she took a creative writing course in high school, she learned that she had been practicing characterization without even knowing it. Her papers always came back with glowing words about how her characters felt alive and real.

Ava opened the fridge and pulled out a cucumber, olives, onions, and chicken. She wanted something fresh and healthy tonight after her walk on the beach and her mother's Greek Chicken recipe sounded like just the thing.

Justin wandered in as she was cutting up the cucumber. "What is that smell?" His eyes darted around as if looking for the source.

"It's balsamic vinegar and chicken. My mother's Greek Chicken recipe." She dumped the cucumber in the bowl with the already sliced Kalamata olives and red onions. Then she turned her attention to the garlic cloves.

"It smells delicious. Greek, huh? Is that your background?"

She began dicing the garlic. "Part. My mother is Greek. My father is Scottish hence the last name McDermott." With a sweep of her hand, she added the garlic to the bowl and checked on the chicken on the stove. It was better when it simmered in a crock pot all day, but as she hadn't thought to start it earlier, she hoped the extra balsamic vinegar would help tenderize the chicken.

"What about you?" she asked as she turned off the stove and retrieved a plate to slice the chicken. "What's your background?"

He looked up from the bowl she had placed her ingredients in. "Uh English. I'm not sure what else." His attention was still fixated on her food. She wondered if he cooked and what he bought for himself at the store.

"Really? You've never been curious? Did you never do one of those family tree things in school?" The chicken looked perfect as her knife sliced through it. Tender and moist. She added the sliced chicken to the bowl and stirred it up with a wooden spoon.

"If I did, I've forgotten about it. I wasn't what you'd call a model student."

Ava glanced up at him. That hardly came as a surprise. She certainly wouldn't have pegged him for one, but that seemed rude to say. "Well, you should some time. It's nice to know your history." She scooped her chicken mixture into a bowl and grabbed a fork from the drawer.

"I don't know why. It's not like I use it as a producer or host." His gaze remained locked on the bowl of food.

"It's not about using it. It's just about having the knowledge. Knowledge is power you know."

He looked up from the bowl. "Money is power."

Ava shook her head as she picked up her bowl and headed to the table. As she sat, she heard the freezer door open. A glance over her shoulder revealed him pulling out a cardboard box. Frozen dinners? That was what he had bought? With a sigh, she shook her head and turned to him. "Don't heat that up. Get yourself a bowl and have some real food."

"Really?"

"Really, but do it quickly before I change my mind."

~

*J*ustin wasted no time in grabbing a bowl and sitting across from her. The smell alone sent him salivating ten minutes ago. He picked up his fork to dig in but Ava interrupted him with her question.

"Frozen dinners?"

He shrugged. "The show I work on caters meals every day. I haven't cooked for myself in months. Besides the store was really small."

Ava chuckled and bowed her head, and Justin knew she was about to pray over her food.

A vice seized his heart, and he forced his eyes to his bowl. He should have known he would get stuck with a believer, and just when he thought Ava might be worth getting to know. He would have to be even more careful about keeping his distance from now on. That was a hole he didn't want to get sucked into again.

"You don't pray?" she asked when she opened her eyes.

"Not anymore. I put my faith in God a long time ago, and He proved He didn't care." Justin dug the fork into the dish and shoveled a mouthful in.

Ava's forehead wrinkled as she picked up her fork. "I

know it feels that way sometimes, but God is always with us."

Justin finished chewing his bite and stared evenly at Ava. "Not when He lets my wife die."

Her mouth dropped open, but he could tell she had no words to say to that. No one ever did. At least not words that mattered. "Thank you for the food, but I think I'll finish it in my room." He stood and carried his plate down the hall. Justin had come here trying to get away from these memories, not dig them up and open old wounds. He wondered, not for the first time, if that would ever be possible.

～

*A*va shut her Bible with a sigh. She had tried blocking out the noise for the last ten minutes, but the words kept bouncing around the page. They had said nothing about quiet time in the evenings, but she would have to tell him to turn the music down. Why on earth did he need it that loud anyway? And why didn't he have headphones?

She grabbed the robe off the end of the bed and shrugged it on. It had been an afterthought to pack it, but now she was glad she had. Her short shorts and tank top revealed too much skin to wear around Justin even though he didn't seem interested in her in the least which she found fine because he was not her type either. This loud blaring rock music emphasized just one of the many differences between them.

Ava knocked lightly at his door and then curled her hand into a fist and pounded when he didn't open up. The music stopped, and the door swung open. Justin wore a tank top himself and a pair of cargo shorts. The casual appearance shocked her for a second, but she should have expected it. No one stayed in slacks and a button-down shirt all day, did they?

"Yes?"

The way his eyes roamed over her sent a heat crawling up her neck, and Ava pulled the robe tighter. "I was hoping you could turn your music down. I'm trying to do my devotional and I can't concentrate with all the screaming going on."

"It's not screaming. It's heavy metal, and it helps me relax."

He moved to shut the door in her face and she shoved her foot out to keep it from closing. "Okay, fair enough, but can you at least turn it down? Or use headphones? I have a pair in my room if you need to borrow some."

Justin sighed and rolled his eyes. "I have my own. I'll use them so you can get back to your fairy tales."

"They're not-" But she didn't get to finish the statement as Justin muscled her foot out of the doorway and shut the door in her face. "You could use some fairy tales," she hissed under her breath as she turned back to her room. He was infuriating and obnoxious, and she tried to cut him slack due to the bomb he had dropped at dinner, but he wasn't making it easy.

At least he kept the music lower. Ava climbed back on the bed and opened her Bible again, but the words still swam over the page. This time it wasn't due to his music but her conscience. With a sigh, she closed the book and then closed her eyes. It was obvious Justin could use prayer and she could use patience dealing with him.

CHAPTER 6

*J*ustin woke early as he did every morning. The filming schedule didn't always call for an early morning wake up but it did more often than not, and his body had gotten used to it. Besides, early morning was always a good time for a run. The sun's rays dispelled less heat then, and fewer people roamed the streets. Of course he didn't have to worry about people out this morning. Other than Ava, the beach seemed deserted, and he'd heard no sound from her room.

He pulled on his shoes and opened his door. A stillness filled the house. Yep, she was definitely still sleeping. For the briefest of moments, he wondered what she looked like when she slept. Did she sleep on the right or left side? Did her hair splay across her pillow?

Justin shook his head to clear the thoughts and inserted the earbuds. Thoughts of Ava had no place in his head. In fact, no woman had a place in his thoughts. He was done with women, and as soon as he found another job outside the dating show, that would be a lot easier.

He pulled open the front door and exited the cottage. This was his favorite time of day, when the sky was still dark and the sun just peeked over the horizon. As he ran, he felt the stress leave his shoulders. Too bad he couldn't get paid to run.

When the sun was fully awake and sweat drenched his shirt, he headed back to the cottage. He would shower and get some breakfast. Then he could spend some time searching out new jobs.

He was surprised to find the cottage still dark when he returned. It was nearly eight a.m. and she had claimed she worked best in the morning. Justin wondered what her definition of morning was. He'd always been an early riser even in his teenage years. When his friends slept in until noon on the weekends, he would be up at seven working out or writing screen plays. His mother had often joked that he must have been a farmer in a previous life because his internal alarm clock seemed to follow the sun. Justin didn't think he would like farm work, but he didn't mind being awake when the rest of the world slept.

Her door was still closed when he got out of the shower and neither the smell of coffee nor the eggs and bacon he cooked seemed to rouse her either. He wondered briefly if he should check to make sure she was still alive, but he was enjoying the quiet. Besides, she would probably take that as another intrusion, and he could use the peace to do some research.

◯

*A*va woke to the sun filtering in her windows. She yawned and stretched. Another long day of writing loomed ahead of her, but at least Justin provided her with plenty of character fodder.

She was still processing the bombshell he'd dropped last night. Death was hard to process even for Christians, but she wondered if his antipathy towards God was just about his wife's death or if there was more to it? Still, she couldn't believe people could look at the world around them and not see God's hand in it all.

After dressing, she grabbed the stack of papers she had made notes on last night. Sometimes her mind worked best with her fingers on the keys, and sometimes it took holding a pen to make the words flow.

Justin sat at the kitchen table when she entered. His laptop took up the majority of the small table leaving Ava with little room.

"You know there are other places you could put your computer so that others could eat breakfast." She opened the fridge and pulled out two eggs and the package of bacon.

"You overslept." His eyes didn't waver from the screen, not even a glance her direction. "It's nine thirty which I'm fairly certain qualifies as morning time. Your best writing time which means you should be in the main room. That makes the kitchen available right now."

"But I haven't eaten yet." Ava tried to keep the

frustration from her voice as she pulled out a skillet and placed two strips of bacon on.

"That's not my problem. You're the one who set the schedule and picked the times if I remember correctly."

He had her there, but Ava wasn't used to such a rigid schedule. Her book had deadlines, but how she got there never followed a strict guideline. She wrote when she felt like it, when the words came. "I did, but that was really more a suggestion of when my best writing time usually is."

Justin did look up at her then - like she had grown a third head. "A schedule is just that, scheduled out blocks of time. Those aren't suggestions."

Okay, so he was a stickler for time. She'd make a note of that and set an alarm clock from now on. He was obviously not a creative mind like herself. "You know you might enjoy the world a little more if you relaxed a little."

"I am relaxed."

"Yes, I can see that from your appearance. By the way, you have an Alfalfa cowlick thing going on today." She smiled as his hand shot to his head and patted his hair. "Yeah, definitely relaxed."

He glared at her, but the bacon began to sizzle then, the heavy aroma filling the air, and she turned her attention to the skillet. When the strips were sufficiently brown and crispy, she transferred them to a plate to cool and then cooked her eggs. A few minutes later, she added them to the plate and returned to the table. There was just enough room for her plate. She said a quick prayer and then picked up her fork.

"What are you working on anyway? If you don't mind me asking."

His response was an irritated stare. "Not that it's any of your business, but I'm looking for new employment opportunities."

"Why? Don't you like being the host of a reality dating show?" Ava didn't watch reality television. She rarely watched television at all unless she was low on ideas and needed some inspiration, but Justin seemed like the perfect host.

Every hair lay in place as if trained meticulously, his skin glowed that nice shade of brown that looked like the sun blessed him though Ava would bet it came from time spent in a tanning bed - she hadn't seen any streaks, so if it came from a bottle, he was good at applying it. Plus, his teeth glistened in the same way the quartz rocks did she often found by the water. Veneers probably. She doubted anyone's teeth were that perfect naturally. Her own dentist kept pushing her to do veneers, but Ava not only liked her slightly crooked bottom tooth, but hated the thought of sanding her teeth to a pulp only to put some artificial cover on them. In fact, maybe she needed to find a new dentist who didn't pitch that offer at her during every visit.

"It's fine, but I want something more, something bigger. When Peter and I first had the idea for the show, I thought I'd be there a year, maybe two and then it would springboard me on to a larger platform."

"How long has it been?" Ava picked up a piece of bacon and took a bite.

"Ten years."

Ava almost choked on her bacon. "Ten years? How does a dating show last that long?"

Justin shrugged and his eyes fell back to the screen. "I suppose there are a lot of people out there looking for love."

Ava couldn't contain her curiosity. "Are you?" She told herself it was research, nothing more, but she found herself holding her breath as she waited for his answer.

"Looking for love?" His eyes flicked briefly to hers and then he shook his head. "No, love and I aren't really on the same page."

Ava wanted to ask why, but she kept her mouth closed. Was it because of his wife? Had there been love after her? Or maybe it went all the way back to his childhood. A divorce of his parents, an affair, a thousand different reasons raced through her mind. Whatever it was, her imagination was probably more interesting than his reality.

"What about you?" He stared at her again, this time with one of those expressions like he was trying to figure out what she was thinking. She almost laughed out loud. Her head was a dangerous place to be with all the thoughts and storylines jockeying for position. She doubted he would enjoy the experience.

"Me? Well, I'm a romance author, so I'm always looking for love."

Justin snorted and turned back to his laptop. "Figures."

Her grip tightened on her fork. "What does that mean?"

"It just figures you would write sappy love stories. You seem like an optimist."

"And what's wrong with being an optimist?" Her hackles rose up, the need to defend herself and her occupation taking over.

"Um, it's not realistic. There are no happy endings just happy moments you might get to enjoy before life comes and slaps them away."

Ava shook her head. "Wow, who stole the color from your rainbows?"

His face wrinkled in confusion. "What?"

"I just mean that's a terrible view on life. How do you work on a dating show with that outlook?" He said nothing and the pieces fell into place. "Oh, so that's why you want to leave, isn't it? You can't stand watching others find happiness."

"Fleeting happiness," he said rolling his eyes. "They usually only last six months before they break up."

"All of them?" Ava found that hard to believe. Even on a dating show, there had to be a few who found lasting happiness. "None have lasted?"

He stared at her as if he couldn't believe she would ask such a stupid question. That third head had probably grown a third eye. "Fine, two of them have."

Ava smiled smugly. "And what did those two couples have that the others didn't?"

"Who knows? Luck more than likely," he said, but his

eyes had shifted. He was lying. Or at least not telling the whole truth. He either knew or suspected what kept those couples together but didn't want to share, and Ava wondered why.

"You better get to writing. It's almost ten, and I can't promise to be quiet after lunch." Before she could respond, he shut his laptop and left the room.

Ava smiled as she finished her breakfast. He was right, and he'd spurred her creative juices enough she thought it would be a very productive couple of hours.

CHAPTER 7

$\mathcal{J}$ ustin stretched out in the hammock and let the gentle rocking blow the troubles from his mind. How long had it been since he'd been able to do nothing and relax? He'd spent a month in Maui which most people would have considered a vacation, but he couldn't remember walking the beach just for fun. No, he'd walked the beach looking for the best places to set up a camera or how the light affected a shot. He'd probably heard the gentle lapping of the waves behind him but he certainly hadn't listened to them as he was now.

Each ebb and flow seemed to have a story. The sands would be arranged just right but then the water would wash ashore and sift them, change them, steal some back to its murky depths. He felt like the sand and life was his ocean.

When he'd first graduated from acting school, dreams

filled his head. Dreams of making it big, of presenting visual stories that people would love, but then he'd met Carol. Suddenly his dreams of making it big shifted. He still desired that but even more he needed a steady income to offer her some stability. That's when he met Peter. A reality dating show hadn't sounded terrible and the audience appeared to be there.

But then Carol had died and his plans had changed again. He'd thrown himself completely into the show needing it to do well in order to keep busy and avoid thinking about Carol. The show's popularity rose and with it his fame which was how he'd met Candy. He should have known with a name like that she wouldn't last, but he'd been lonely and foolish. However, she had been the wave that took a piece of him back to her murky depth.

Now he felt lost, adrift in the sea of life without a compass. He hoped a new gig would give him focus, something to work toward but he wasn't even sure of that. The only thing he was sure of was that he felt even more like the sand, like he was at the mercy of the waves, and at any moment, they might arise and tear down his carefully built castles.

His phone buzzed in his pocket, and a terrible feeling it held a wave washed over him. Peter's number on the screen came as no surprise, but that knowledge didn't warm the chill that was slowly spreading through his veins.

"Hello?"

"Justin. It's Peter. How is the stay going?"

"Well, it's only day two, but I'm working on relaxing. Lying in a hammock right now listening to the waves. However, they made a mistake when you booked and I'm having to share the cottage with a woman."

"A woman?"

"Yeah, some romance writer. There are no other cottages available and the contract says we have to wait three days before asking for a refund."

"What is she like?"

"The woman?" Why on earth would Peter care what this woman was like?

"Yes, the woman, who else?"

Justin glanced back at the cottage. "She's infuriating. Always looks for the positive, believes in love, and prays before every meal, so not really my type. Not that I'm looking for romance."

"Is she pretty?"

Why was he pushing this? Hadn't Justin told him she wasn't his type? "I suppose." In truth, she was pretty, and Justin had noticed. Her raven hair made her skin appear creamy and soft and her green eyes held just the hint of a challenge when she stared at him. "Why do you ask? I thought I was supposed to be relaxing and not thinking about some woman. At least that's what my *boss* told me." Justin made sure to put extra emphasis on the word boss.

"Partners, Justin. We're in this together."

Right. Except that Justin didn't think he could send Peter on a mandatory pull-yourself-together retreat. There were clearly areas where Peter held the control, but that was an argument for another day. "All right, partner, what is this call really about? I don't believe you called just to check up on me."

Peter sighed on the other end of the phone. "It's your image, Justin. Somehow, they caught wind of what you told Carl and the tabloids are blowing up about it. They're calling you a humbug, a Grinch, and my personal favorite, the male Eris."

Justin scanned his memory of mythology, but the name was just out of reach. "Who was Eris?"

"The goddess of discord. Not a great comparison for a dating show host."

It wasn't, but as Justin wasn't sure he wanted to be a dating show host any longer, he wasn't entirely sure it was as bad as Peter was making it out to be either. "Look, Peter, I know it sounds awful, but I think I might be done with 'Who Wants to Marry a Cowboy.'"

"I think you're missing the point, Justin. This isn't about you looking bad on the show. This is affecting your brand. I've known you were thinking about leaving for a while, but right now you are damaged goods. No show is going to pick you up with this reputation."

And there it was - the wave. He couldn't lose his brand. He was known as the charismatic host, and he needed that to secure another job. "What can I do?"

"You need a rebrand, and you need it quickly. Look, I know you're on personal leave, but you need to find a way to show the world you haven't given up on love, that you aren't starting a one-man crusade to destroy it."

"And how do you suggest I do that?" Marketing had not been Justin's strength in college and he'd taken no classes about remaking your image.

"I can really only think of one thing."

Justin knew he wasn't going to like Peter's answer, but he asked anyway. "What's that?"

"You need to get a girlfriend and quickly."

Justin nearly dropped the phone. "No, uh unh, there has to be another way. I told you I was done dating after Candy."

"I don't mean for love, Justin. I mean for show. You need to find a woman, preferably someone who screams romance and you need to date her. In public. That will be the fastest way to fix your image. They can't say you hate love when you are in a relationship. Then, after you've been together a while, you guys can amicably separate. Have your jobs tear you apart or something, but no big break ups. Do you know of a woman like that?"

A woman who screamed romance. He looked back at the cabin picturing Ava sitting in the big chair. "Like a romance author?"

"Now you're talking. Do you think she'll do it?"

"I don't know; I just met her yesterday. How do I get her to agree?"

"Give her something she wants. Make it a deal she can't refuse."

A deal she couldn't refuse. He had no idea what that

would even be. He supposed it was time he started
warming up to her.

~

*A*va read back over her words with a sigh. They
were fine, but that was it. They were just fine.
There was no spark, no sizzle. She had thought coming
here would help her be inspired, but though the words
were coming, they weren't doing anything fantastic. There
was no dancing on the page or jumping out at you. They
just marched in single file and stood at attention. Maybe
Genevieve would have some insight. Ava pulled out her cell
phone and punched in the familiar number.

"Hey you, how's the writing going?" Gen had picked
up before the phone rang twice in Ava's ear. She was fairly
certain Genevieve had a psychic streak. She always seemed
to know who was on the other end before she picked up
the phone.

"Not great. I mean I wrote a lot but the words aren't
magical. They're just standing there doing nothing."

"It's because you need to experience. I told you that life
isn't perfect. You need to get out a little and date more."

"I think it's more because the rental lady double
booked the cottage and I'm having to share it with a living
Ken doll."

"What?"

"Yeah, evidently there was some mix up and she
booked me and this dating show host at the same time, and

he is a piece of work. Doesn't believe in love, listens to heavy metal, hates God. You know pretty much the opposite of me."

"Is he cute?"

Ava shook her head. "Why? I just told you he's the opposite of me."

"I know, but hear me out, Ava. I forgot to remind you, but the annual romance gala is tomorrow night. It would be so much better for your image if you actually brought a date this year."

Ava clapped her hand to her forehead. She had forgotten all about the gala, and she dreaded those events. Last year, she had attended without a date and received pitying looks all night. "Wait, are you saying I should take Justin?"

"If you could handle him for a night, then I think it would be better than going alone again."

The front door opened, and Justin entered, looking a little like a cat who had eaten a canary. Ava wasn't even sure what it was - the glint in his eye, the smile that looked almost genuine, the air of excitement that floated by his head, but something had obviously happened while he was out.

"I'll call you back." She pressed the end call button before Genevieve could say anything else.

"Sorry I didn't mean to interrupt."

"It's fine. It was just my editor. We talk nearly every day anyway."

He bit his lip and nodded. "How's the writing going?"

It wasn't the question he wanted to ask - she could tell by the way he shifted from one foot to the other. The shift was subtle, but she was a people watcher.

"It's been better. I have words, but they aren't doing anything."

"Would you like some help? I'd be happy to read some."

Ava's brow furrowed. Why was he being so nice? "You? The man who hates romance?"

He shrugged. "Maybe the fresh air is doing me good."

"I don't think so. I think there's something else, so why don't you tell me what you really want."

Justin sighed and held up his finger in a 'give-me-a-minute' gesture. He disappeared into the kitchen and then returned with one of the chairs sitting it a little too close for Ava's comfort.

"What's the one thing you want most in this world?" He reached for her hands but then seemed to think better of it and folded them in his lap.

"You mean besides world peace?" What was wrong with him? Had he found wild mushrooms? Someone selling special brownies?

"I'm serious. If you could have anything in the world, what would it be?"

"Chocolate mousse from Paris. My friend went once and she said it was divine." Frustration creased his face and he sat back and ran a hand through his hair. Ava rolled her eyes. She didn't know what bug had bitten him, but he was wound tighter than Dick's hatband as her momma used to say. "Okay, fine. I guess I'd want to be a successful author. Have more people read my books and maybe change their hearts."

He leaned forward so fast she thought he might fly out of the chair and this time his hands did find hers. She doubted he even noticed though because his eyes danced like a flickering candle flame and his features were more animated than she'd thought possible from him.

"That's what I'm talking about. Now, what if I could make that happen?"

He had gone off the deep end. Ava gently removed her hands from his and leaned away from him. "Are you a genie now granting wishes? I don't see your lamp anywhere."

"Of course not. I only play one on tv." He flashed a teasing smile. This was a side she hadn't seen of him, but then she'd just met him yesterday. He probably had many sides she hadn't seen. "But seriously, if I could make that happen, would you do me a favor?"

Ah, now he was getting to the real question though what favor she could do for him she had no idea. "I guess it depends on what the favor is."

His shoulders rose and fell in an exaggerated gesture as if gathering courage for whatever was about to come out of his mouth. "Okay, hear me out. I know we just met, but I need you to be my girlfriend."

If Ava'd had a drink in her mouth, she would have spat the contents all over him. Instead, a surprised chuckle escaped Ava's mouth. Then it grew and became a full-fledged throaty laugh. He really had lost his mind. Only he wasn't laughing. Why wasn't he laughing? Her laugh died in her throat. "You're serious," she said when she was able to speak again.

"I am. I just got a call from my boss and it turns out that my lackluster feelings about love were discovered."

"Imagine that," Ava interrupted, but Justin continued as if he hadn't heard her.

"I'm all over the media and not in a good way. It's important we turn my image around fast, and Peter's suggestion was a romance."

"Then Peter is crazier than you are." Ava stood and began pacing the room. "And why me? You don't even know me. Don't you have some female friend you could ask? Surely, you haven't soured all the women you've met."

Justin's jaw clenched at her words, and he stood as well. "I'm kind of a loner. I don't have a lot of close friends, much less girl friends."

"Well, color me surprised. You mean that surly attitude of yours doesn't have women falling at your feet?" That information did not surprise Ava in the least.

Again, he let her comment slide. He must really need her help. "Besides, it needs to be someone who screams romance. Someone the public will love. Who better at romance than a romance author?"

Ava covered her face with her hands. This couldn't be happening. She had come here hoping to find quiet to finish her novel not jump into a fake relationship with some stranger. "I don't even know you. What do we even have in common?"

"We both like the ocean," he said gesturing out the window. "And Code Red Mountain Dew."

Ava threw her hands up in frustration. "We cannot build a relationship on a carbonated beverage."

Justin shook his head. "A fake relationship, and we can build it on anything. We can make up some fantastical story if you'd like. Look, you help me turn my image around. In return, I help put you on the map. We'll get tons of press, some tv interviews. You'll be a household name and your books will fly off the shelves."

Ava couldn't believe she was even considering this, but her books getting exposure was her dream. And exposure like this? It would be years before she could afford something like this. Plus, there was the gala. She would have a date. Of course it would only be a good thing if he could pretend to enjoy romance, but he was a television host. He must have some acting skills. "How long are we talking? I mean I do hope to marry for love one day in the future, and that requires being free to date."

"A few weeks. Maybe a month. We just need to attend events, score a few interviews, be seen together. Peter thinks that should be long enough to turn my image around and make it believable and then we amicably separate. Claim our work pulled us apart or something like that as long as there's no public fighting."

When he put it that way, it did sound much more like a business arrangement than a relationship, and she would get things she needed in return. "I need to think about it and call my editor back."

"Of course." The excited mania left Justin's face and he reverted back to his plasticky, used car salesman look.

Could she really pretend to be in a relationship with someone who reminded her of a used car salesman?

CHAPTER 8

*A*va stared at the phone wondering how the call would go. "Hey Gen, you know that guy I'm sharing the cottage with? He just proposed faking a relationship with me." Yeah, it sounded stupid even to her ears, but perhaps Gen would have sound advice for her.

"Hey, Ava." She picked up before it even rang on Ava's side. Psychic ability for sure. "You going to tell my why you hung up on me?"

Yep, right to the chase. That was Genevieve for you. "Justin came in."

"Oh?" It was only one word, but Ava could almost envision Gen as she said it. Her left eyebrow would be arched high on her forehead, her right eye would be a little squinty, and she would have dropped whatever she was doing or sat up straight in her chair.

"Yeah, he wanted to run something by me."

"And?" How? How did she always know there was more?

"And he just offered me a strange proposal." There. She'd said it. And it still sounded ridiculous. Maybe even more so out loud.

"What? He proposed?" Ava smiled at the surprise in Gen's voice. Finally, she had shocked her friend. In the three years she had known Genevieve, Ava had never shocked her until now. And then Gen's words translated in her brain.

"No, not proposed. Not like marriage anyway. He wants me to pretend to be his girlfriend."

"Why?" Gen's voice had shifted to her inquisitive, what's-the-deal tone, and Ava could picture the expression on her face. "Did you tell him about the gala?" She was glad she was doing this over the phone and not in person because she'd probably be squirming under Gen's scrupulative gaze right about now.

"Not yet. He needs his image fixed. Specifically, his image on love. He's the host of some reality dating show, but I guess someone caught wind that he's not big on romance. His boss thinks a romance could save that, and Justin says he can get exposure for my books through television spots and the works."

"This is perfect, Ava."

"It is?" Perfect was not the word Ava would have chosen to describe her and Justin.

"Yes, you agree to this fake relationship and you can take him to the gala. A romance writer with a boyfriend improves your image. Plus, he's for real. I'm googling him right now and he really is somebody, not A-list celebrity status but enough that he might get some interviews. This could be amazing for your books."

"Yeah, but do you think people will believe it? We are total opposites remember?"

"People believe anything you put in front of them if you sell it right. And opposites attract. It's like the greatest love story trope of all time."

Ava bit her lip. What Gen was saying made sense, but a fake relationship? She prided herself on truth and honesty. "I don't know, Gen. It's lying."

"Yeah, but it's not hurting anyone. You help his image, he helps yours. It's a win for everyone."

"I suppose you're right and people will look me up and my books. This is the kind of exposure I could never buy, and it's only for a few weeks." Ava wasn't sure if the words coming out of her mouth were to convince Genevieve or herself.

"I think it's perfect. The only thing is…. Your mom. Have you thought of what you're going to tell your mother?"

Her mother. There was the rub. Her parents had been high school sweethearts. They had dated no one else, and they believed in true love. Ava doubted her parents would approve, but she was thirty years old, and this was her decision to make and not theirs.

"I'll tell her what we tell everyone else. It was love at first sight."

*J*ustin ran a hand across his forehead as he stared at the laptop. It was as bad as Peter had claimed. Infamy sometimes worked in an actor's favor, but it rarely worked in the favor of a host or producer who was known for love stories. And even though he wasn't sure he wanted to continue down that path, if he didn't get his image fixed, the only thing he would be working on were dark depressing shows.

A change down that path might be okay for a while, but he knew those dark shows wore on the people who worked on them as well. He had known a lot of actors and writers who had left shows like CSI and Law and Order because they carried their work home. No, he wanted the flexibility to be able to change and work where he wanted, but that meant fixing his image.

What if Ava said no? It was crazy of him to even assume she might say yes seeing as how they had only met yesterday, but he had no one else in his pocket. He might be able to find a desperate model or actress, but he'd had his fill of pretentious, self-centered women. Ava didn't seem to possess any of those vices. She really was the best current choice, and she was certainly easy on the eyes. They probably wouldn't have to be affectionate very often, but he could see himself kissing her if necessary. And that wouldn't be the worst thing in the world.

The floor creaked, and he looked up to see Ava standing in the doorway. She'd left to call her editor and ponder his offer. Had she decided then? He tried to find the decision in her face - a twinkle in her eyes, the set of her mouth, but there was nothing. She would make a great poker player. "Hey, Ava." He would tread lightly. If she wasn't firm in her decision, maybe he could convince her to change her mind.

"Justin." She sat across from him and held his gaze.

He felt as if he were at a chess match and they were engaged in a battle of wits. Though it pained him on every level, he waited for her to say more. Time seemed to stand still as they stared at each other. The sound of his heart pumping thudded in his head and from somewhere came a soft ticking sound like a second hand of a watch or clock.

"I've considered your offer." She was being just as laconic as he was. Was she playing the same game?

"And?" His breath caught in his throat stilled by her penetrating gaze.

Tiny flecks of gold danced in the bright green of her irises as her eyes bore into his. "And I accept."

Elation flooded Justin and he fought to keep from breaking out in a wide grin. There was no need to let Ava know how much this meant to him. It would diminish the value of his bargaining chips regarding the rules he was about to lay down. "Great. If we're going to do this, we need some ground rules." Never one to do anything without planning, he had spent the last few minutes ruminating on how it would work and some basic rules to make sure it proceeded as planned.

"Ground rules?" Ava asked. "Why can't we just wing it? Won't that seem more natural?"

Wing it? Was she serious? This was his future they were talking about. "No, we cannot wing it. The media are like dogs. If they spot an irregularity in our story, they will latch onto it and research it until they find the truth. If it was found out this was only a ruse, it could destroy both of our names."

"Okay, okay," Ava held up her hands in surrender. "What are your rules?"

"Rule number one, other than Peter and your editor-"

"Genevieve," she supplied.

"Right her. Other than those two, we tell no one this isn't real. The fewer people that know about it, the safer our secret is."

"Okay, what else?"

He glanced down at his list. "We will have to go on some dates. It would raise flags if we announced this relationship but were never seen together."

"How many is some?"

"I'm not sure. We can play that part by ear, and I'll pay. It wouldn't help my image on love if I expected you to pay."

"Okay, can I choose one of the dates because I kind of have a thing I need you for?"

"Oh?" How did she already have something she needed him for? He had just offered this solution a half hour ago.

Her eyes dropped to the table top and followed her

index finger as it traced a pattern he couldn't see. "It's a romance gala. Fancy dinner, some dancing, awards. Last year I went alone, but that doesn't really work in a romance writer's favor. So, can we make that one of the dates?"

Justin ran a hand across his chin. He wasn't a fan of fancy affairs, but there would probably be press there. It might be the perfect place to reveal their relationship. "Yeah, I suppose."

"There's just one thing. It's tomorrow night, so we'll have to cut our stay short. I guess we won't have to ask Margie for that refund after all. Is that still okay?"

As much as he didn't want to head back to work early, he did need to save his image. "Sure, but can I ask you one thing?"

Ava shrugged. "I guess."

"Why are you alone? I mean romance hasn't been good to me, but you write about it, so you must still like it."

Ava's lips pulled into a small smile. "It's my parents' fault. They have this amazing relationship, and that's what I grew up seeing." She shrugged and sighed. "I just don't want to settle for less, and I haven't found that perfect romance yet."

Justin could understand that. He respected that. His parents hadn't had the best relationship, but that had pushed him to want to have a great one when he did. And he had. With Carol. Until life took her from him. "That makes sense. I'm sorry you haven't found what you're looking for yet."

She blinked at him. "You are? You? The man who hates romance?"

He rolled his eyes. "I didn't always hate romance." However, he was done talking about it. "Here's what I've come up with so far. We'll have dinner-"

"Where?" Ava asked interrupting him.

"It doesn't matter," he said waving his hand, "somewhere public."

"Um, it certainly does matter. A hot dog stand is public but not romantic. If people are going to believe we are in a relationship, we need romantic dates."

Justin sighed and rubbed a hand across his forehead. Peter had better be right about this. "Fine, what do you suggest?"

"I guess that depends on where you live. I live in Glendale, and we have a great Italian restaurant there, Genaro's."

Justin knew the place. It was pricey, but it would be a good place to be seen. "Fine, I'll see if I can get a reservation there in the next few days. I live in West Hollywood, so I'm not far from you."

"Great, what else do you have planned?"

"I'm hoping to score us an interview and then a movie night. Maybe something on the boardwalk where celebrities are known to pass by. I can plan the rest later once we see how the public responds to us."

Ava took a deep breath. "Can I ask one thing?" Justin nodded. "This relationship is in name only, right? You don't expect me to perform," she paused as she bit her lip, "girlfriend duties, do you?"

Girlfriend duties? What did that even mean? He chuckled slightly before he could stop himself. She sounded like someone from the fifties. "No, no girlfriend duties." He couldn't even say the word without chuckling. "We may have to hold hands, kiss a few times for the camera, but that's it."

A blush colored her cheeks when he said the word kiss. "Okay, I think you have yourself a deal. So, where do we go from here?"

Justin smiled and laid out his vision for the next step.

CHAPTER 9

"Okay, so I guess all that's left is for us to practice a kiss," Justin said as he pushed back his chair and stood. He walked to the fridge and pulled out a drink as if this was the most normal statement in the world.

Ava blinked at him. She must have misunderstood the words that came from his mouth. "I'm sorry. You want to do what?"

He rolled his eyes at her as he unscrewed the cap and took a drink. "Practice a kiss. People will expect to see one somewhere along the line. I've watched enough actors to know that if we don't practice this, it will look fake. Hounds, remember?"

"Won't it look more natural if we just do it when it comes up though?"

He shook his head. "No, it will look like an awkward first kiss. We don't want to look awkward. Maybe hounds isn't a good analogy. Maybe you should think about the press like sharks who attack when they smell blood. In our case, the blood would be anything that seems off. Like an awkward first kiss."

He took a step toward her, and Ava gripped the sides of the seat. She should stand. This wouldn't work if she stayed sitting, but her legs refused to work. Her heart, however, thudded in her chest. "Sharks, right." It wasn't that she didn't kiss. It was just that it had been a while since she had kissed. There was a part of her that thought she might be rusty if such a thing existed.

Justin set his water down on the table and held out his hand. Ava noticed hers trembling as she placed it in his. He pulled her to her feet with ease, but her legs still felt like Jell-O. How did he look so calm when her gut was a twisted bundle of nerves? Then his hand touched her cheek. It was soft and not entirely unpleasant. His eyes stared into hers and she wondered how long it had been for him? He seemed so rigid toward romance. Would he kiss the same? Stiff and thought out as he seemed to do everything.

He leaned closer and her breath caught. Should she tilt her head? Would their noses bump? Why did she feel like a teen experiencing her first kiss?

His face was close enough she could feel the warmth emanating from his mouth. She closed her eyes and his lips touched hers. Tentative at first as if exploring her response then they pressed harder and Ava felt the need behind them. She responded and found her arms circling his neck.

Her eyes opened when he pulled back. She felt dizzy,

like the room was spinning. His hands pulled her arms from his neck. They stayed on her upper arms a moment as if to steady her before falling to his side. She immediately missed the warmth they had offered.

"I think we'll be fine." His voice was husky and his eyes cloudy. He ran a hand over his chin as he stepped back. And not just a normal step back. He took a large step as if he feared she had a contagious disease. Had he not liked the kiss? Or had he, like her, been more affected by it than he'd thought he would be?

⁓

Fine? He was not fine. Fine did not explain the heat searing across his lips or the pounding of his heart in his head. It was not an adequate word to describe the flames of desire that had coursed through his body when his lips touched hers nor the lingering flickers that erupted at the mere thought of kissing her again. And it certainly didn't justify the traitorous thoughts racing through his head right now. Thoughts of a real relationship with Ava. Thoughts of opening his heart again. No, it was just a kiss. There were too many differences between them.

He turned from her questioning gaze. His behavior probably confused her, but that's because it confused him as well. He hadn't expected to feel anything with that kiss. He had expected it to be methodical, emotionless, awkward even. After all, this relationship wasn't real. It was a show for the media to improve his image and increase her sales. That's all it was. Or all it was supposed to be.

A loud sigh escaped his lips as he pulled the front door open. Fresh air. He needed a breath of fresh air to clear his head.

The warmth rolled over him as he stepped into the sun, but the peace didn't last long. Justin pulled his cell phone out of his pocket and answered the incoming call.

"Hey, Peter."

"Justin, how are things going with your author friend?"

Friend? That was a loaded word. "Good. She agreed to do it. We've been hashing out the details so our stories align and we're attending a Romance Gala tomorrow night."

"Good, I leaked the information and The Evening Show wants to do an interview. Can you two be there Saturday night?"

"Yeah, it shouldn't be a problem." A gala tomorrow and an interview the day after. That didn't give him much time to get his emotions under control, but he could do it. He would just have to avoid touching her because he was fairly certain he would not be able to control himself if he did.

CHAPTER 10

*A*va closed her eyes and touched her finger to her lips. They still throbbed from Justin's kiss. How could someone who drove her so crazy affect her so much?

It must be the situation, the whole insane fake relationship idea had her mind spinning in a direction it had never been in before, but she could use this. She could write the romance scene while it was fresh in her mind.

She opened her laptop and let her fingers fly over the keyboard. It had been a long time since a romantic scene flowed this easily for her. Perhaps Gen had been right.

The door opened and Justin stepped back in, but he didn't even glance at her. He walked straight to his room, and a moment later, the loud thumping sound of his heavy metal music poured out ending her writing time. At least for now. No matter, she had gotten down several thousand words and she could always finish later.

After shutting the screen, she grabbed her sunglasses and headed for the front door. If she had to leave tomorrow, at least she could take some time to enjoy the ocean a little longer today.

"Oh, Margie," she said in surprise when she opened the door and saw the elderly woman on the porch. "What can I do for you?"

"I just thought I would check on you and Justin. See how things were going." She peeked around Ava as if trying to see inside the cottage.

Ava shielded the doorway though she didn't know why except that she found it odd that Margie was checking up on them. "Um, things are fine. We both have to return home tomorrow, so I guess we won't be bothering you about the refund after all."

Margie's expression took on a look of concern. "It's nothing serious I hope."

"No, just work obligations we had forgotten about."

"Ah, well, sometimes the timing just isn't right. Perhaps you two can return when the timing is better."

"Yes, perhaps." Ava watched Margie get in her car and drive away before shutting the door behind her. The woman was sweet but definitely an odd one.

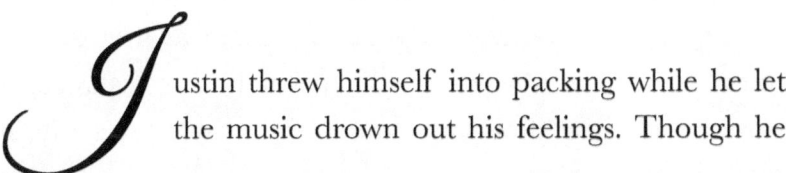

*J*ustin threw himself into packing while he let the music drown out his feelings. Though he was cutting his vacation short, he was glad they would be leaving tomorrow. After that kiss, he wanted to put some distance between himself and Ava.

He tried to think about why the kiss had affected him so badly as he folded each article of clothing and placed them back in his bag. Was it because they were so different? Because she irritated him? That had to be it. The passion in the kiss had come from their mutual dislike of each other. That happened, right? He just needed to remind himself that they would never work. She was too different; he was too broken. As long as he remembered that, he should be fine.

Justin stayed in his room until dinner. He didn't want to chance seeing Ava. When he did emerge, it was with a list of things to talk about. He wanted no moment of silence that would force him to think about that kiss.

She was at the table eating a plate of spaghetti when he entered the kitchen. "There's extra on the stove," she said motioning with her head.

"Thank you. I made a list of a few things we should discuss before we head out tomorrow." He grabbed a plate from the cupboard and filled it. The smell of garlic and olives reached his nose and his stomach rumbled.

"Okay, like what?"

"We should exchange numbers. We need a way to keep in contact, and we should probably share a little of our interests in case we get asked separately. For instance, it would look bad if I said you loved strawberries but it turned out you were allergic."

Ava nodded and took another bite. "Makes sense. I'm not allergic to strawberries since you asked. In fact, I love chocolate covered strawberries."

Justin would have made a comment about how cliché that was but he also loved chocolate covered strawberries.

"I am, however, allergic to shellfish. In fact, I don't eat seafood at all."

"And I love seafood." This was good. More differences between them just solidified why they didn't belong together. If he could keep this going, he could put that kiss out of his mind. Except that he couldn't because every time she took a bite, her mouth drew his attention.

He doubted she had any idea, but she ate food in a way he had never seen anyone eat before. Almost seductively. Each bite was slow and deliberate as if she was really tasting every morsel, and she didn't shove her fork in. Instead it appeared to glide over her lips, deliver the bite, and then ease out the same way. Every once in a while, her eyes would flicker and then close a touch longer than a blink. He found the whole experience… cute.

"What?" Ava had stopped eating and was staring at him.

A smile tugged at the corners of his lips. "You eat seductively."

"I eat what?" A pink blush spread across her cheeks.

"Seductively. Like every bite might be your last." He chuckled at the horrified expression on her face before realizing what he had just done. He'd flirted with her, and he could not do that. He would not do that. "Anyway, we can share more through text. I'm going to finish this in my room." He pushed back from the chair like someone had lit a fire under his seat. His rude behavior was confusing, but it was the only protection he had. So, he was going to use it.

CHAPTER 11

*A*va should be writing. Her story still wasn't complete. She had written a little more, but the image of that kiss kept popping into her mind. That kiss that was supposed to mean nothing but obviously meant something because he had left right after and when he'd come back, he'd avoided her eyes and kept a greater than usual distance the rest of the time at the cottage.

So now she was more confused. Navigating a fake relationship posed a new challenge on its own. But that kiss had changed things. It had transformed a relationship designed to end into something that might be real. How was she supposed to navigate through those mine-infested waters? What were the rules for that? Were there even rules?

She shut the laptop screen. As much as she wanted to write, tonight was their first official date - the gala, and she needed to get ready.

A knock sounded at her front door. Genevieve was right on time. Ava might be the writer, but Gen had the better fashion sense, so Ava often asked her to approve any final look before events that might have cameras.

"You're not even dressed?" Gen asked as Ava pulled the door open.

"Hello to you too. No, I was trying to write and drawing a blank as usual." She stepped back and Genevieve entered, makeup case in her hand.

"Well, perhaps tonight will help spur your creativity. If you let it. Now, when does Justin arrive?"

Ava checked her watch. "Uh, an hour."

"We better get started then."

Ava followed Gen to her bedroom. The dress, a slinky red one-shouldered number, lay across her bed.

"Ooh, nice choice," Gen said. "Red for the win."

"I thought it might say love better than black."

"Oh, it does. Plus, it will look amazing with your dark hair and creamy complexion. Justin will fall for you for real when I'm done with you."

Ava's fingers stole to her lips. She could still feel his lips on hers. It had been a long time since she had felt heat like that.

Gen's eyes widened. "What aren't you telling me?"

Ava pulled her hand from her lips and looked away. "Nothing."

"Un unh, that look is not nothing," Gen said shaking her head in that you-can't-fool-me fashion. "Clearly something happened while you guys were there and I want details."

A sigh burst forth from Ava's lips as she sank onto her pillow top bed. "Okay, we kissed."

Gen's eyes widened to half dollars. "I'm sorry, you did what?"

"We kissed. It wasn't supposed to mean anything, but he wanted to practice so our first kiss didn't look awkward."

The corners of Gen's lips twitched. "I'm going to guess awkward wouldn't describe it."

Ava's lips burned as the scene replayed itself in her head. "I'm not sure awkward is the word I would use, but it ended so quickly and he avoided me after, so it might be my imagination making it something it wasn't."

"Somehow I doubt that, but I guess you'll find out tonight." Gen glanced down at her watch. "And we're running out of time, so we better get to it."

Ava nodded as she pushed herself off the bed and tried to erase the image of Justin's lips on hers from her mind.

～

Justin looked at the number on his phone one more time. He didn't know what he had expected with her being an author, but it certainly wasn't this modest apartment complex. Not that there was anything wrong with apartments, but he preferred a house where you couldn't hear every sound your neighbors made and you didn't have to share the parking space with eight other people. It made him wonder if she lived here by choice or financial reasons.

He locked the car and approached the landing. Apartment B sat on the right. He rang the bell and smoothed his suit one more time. The door swung open, but it was not Ava on the other side. A pretty redhead smiled at him.

"You must be Justin. I'm Genevieve." Her eyes traveled from his head to his feet before she shrugged as if she expected more but he would do.

"Ah, the editor."

"And friend." She stepped back and opened the door wider for him. "Which is why I get to say this. I know this is a fake relationship, but this is my friend we're talking about and I don't want to see her get hurt." Lightning flashed in her eyes and Justin took an involuntary step back. She might be small, but her gaze was fierce.

"Believe me, I've been down that road before and I have no intention of getting hurt either. I'm not looking for love. We are just helping each other out." But he wondered if that were still true after that kiss. It had been a simple kiss, but it had shaken him to the core. He'd thought he had shut off those feelings after Candy, but it appeared he hadn't.

"Un huh, I've heard that before. Just know that I've got my eye on you." She formed a vee with her fingers and flashed them from her eyes to his.

Justin pressed his lips together to keep from smiling.

Genevieve had spunk, and he liked that, but he wouldn't let her know that. "Understood. Now, is she ready because we will be late if she doesn't hurry."

Genevieve's green eyes danced as her smile deepened. "Oh, she's ready. The question is, are you?"

At that moment, Ava appeared in the doorway behind Genevieve and Justin's jaw dropped. She was a vision. Her dark hair was pulled up on her head with just a few tendrils snaking down the side and resting against her neck. Her neck looked long and slender and as silky as cream as it led to smooth shoulders. One shoulder held a thin strap of red fabric, but the other remained bare. And the dress. It hung perfectly on her frame and showed just the right amount of skin.

"You look..." He had no words. Beautiful wasn't enough. Exotic came close, but it still wasn't right. She was more. More beautiful, more exotic, more whatever than anything he had ever seen.

"I think amazing is the word you're searching for," Genevieve said with a satisfied smile.

No, amazing didn't cut it either, but Justin didn't argue with her.

"Thank you. You look handsome as well." There was no expression of conceit on Ava's face, but a slight pink graced her cheeks as if she weren't used to receiving compliments.

Justin wanted to admire her longer, let his eyes drink in every drop of her, but that was a dangerous path. "Shall we go?" he offered instead hoping the drive to the gala would allow him to get his emotions back under control.

"Can I do one thing first?" She stepped toward him with a gleam in her eye. Before he could say anything, she reached up and tousled his hair. A chill shot down his back at the feel of her fingers on his head. "It looked too perfect, but now it is perfect."

Justin stared into her eyes. He didn't normally let people touch his hair, but it was like he was under a spell around Ava, one he needed to break before he found himself falling for real.

"I'm ready now," she said with a smile as she grabbed a small clutch from a table by the door.

Justin caught Genevieve's smirk before he turned and followed Ava out of the apartment. He quickened his pace to get to his dark blue BMW 8 series coupe first and open the passenger door for her. An expression of awe landed on her face, and he smiled. It was subtle, just the minute parting of her lips and widening of her eyes, but it was there. "This is nice." Her hand ran across the leather seat at her sides.

"Thank you. It's been a dream purchase for years." Decades actually. He had wanted this car before he met Carol, then marrying her had consumed his focus and his money. When she got sick, the money turned into her treatments and then her funeral. Then he had met Candy. He swore she could smell money and had gladly taken half of his money not tied up in assets when she'd left. That put his dreams of purchasing the car on hold again until the divorce was final which was why he still owed as much on the loan as he did. Justin shook his head as he shut Ava's door. He didn't need to walk down memory lane tonight or ever. It was too painful and not helpful at all.

It was all he could do to keep his eyes on the road during the drive to the gala. He could feel Ava beside him, this feminine presence that attacked his senses. Even with his focus straightforward, the red of her dress and the white of her arms and legs danced in his peripheral vision. And a smell like vanilla and sugar filled his nose igniting memories of his mother in the kitchen. He took a deep breath. He needed to get ahold of his runaway thoughts. This was business. Nothing more and he would do well to remember that.

The gala was being held in a large skyrise building that appeared to be almost entirely glass. Even the elevator they took to the top floor was glass except for the metal beams. Watching the ground disappear under his feet was an unnerving experience and sent his stomach twisting. It must not have been enjoyable for Ava as well because she kept her hands firmly on the silver hand rail and her eyes straight ahead. The knuckles on her hands turned white with her death grip.

Relief covered him when the elevator dinged and the doors opened to a hallway with a floor that was not see through. He stepped out relishing the firmness of floors and walls around him - solid walls that held their secrets within. To the right was a table manned by a woman with long blond hair, and as that looked to be the only thing in the short hallway, he headed that direction.

The woman looked like a Barbie even from this far back with her blond hair curled to perfection and a dress tight enough to display her small waist. Justin felt Ava tense beside him. He risked a glance at her surprised to see her jaw clench and a tiny vein in her neck bulge out. There was obviously history between these two and he wondered what it was.

"Ava, so glad you could join us again this year." The Barbie's voice held the sickly-sweet tone of insincerity, and her smile appeared far too practiced. It was a smile Justin knew and performed all too well.

"Thank you, Tia, happy to be here." Ava's voice sounded pinched and tight, but she too kept a smile firmly on her face.

Tia's eyes shifted to Justin and one eyebrow arched slightly. "I see you brought a date this year. How lucky for you. It's *so* great you're finally seeing someone."

Her emphasis on the word so combined with her fake smile rubbed Justin the wrong way, and now it made sense to Justin. Tia was the school bully of the romance world, casting her piteous looks and words on anyone she deemed unworthy. Justin could see the effect it had on Ava in her eyes - the light in them dimmed and the extra glistening told him tears were close. Though he knew touching her might be his undoing, he couldn't stand to see her wilt in front of this viper.

He wrapped an arm around Ava's shoulders and pulled

her to him. "Ava stole my heart from the first moment I saw her. I'm the lucky one." He held Tia's gaze, daring her to challenge him, but she had clearly not expected his words.

She blinked, her long fake eyelashes fanning out on her perfectly blushed cheeks. "Wait, are you Justin Miller from Who Wants to Marry a Cowboy?"

Justin couldn't help puffing his chest out a little. She might be awful, but she had recognized him. "I am."

Her posture stiffened, and she dropped her eyes to the table. Clearly, it bugged her that Ava had shown up with him. "Well, I hope you two have fun." She handed Ava a small name plate and a blank one to Justin. "Just write your name here and set it on your table."

Justin picked up the marker she indicated and penned his name across the blank paper. "I'm sure we will have fun. Every day I get to spend with Ava is better than the day before." He leaned in and kissed Ava's cheek enjoying the shocked expression on Tia's face.

Then, arm still around her, he led her away from the table and into the room. "You didn't have to do that." Ava's voice was small beside him and had he not held her so close, he might not have heard her at all.

"Yeah, I did. I can't stand people like that - the kind that think the only way to feel better about themselves is to make others feel bad about themselves. I may not like many people, but I don't pretend I do either."

She offered him a sincere smile along with a look of gratitude. "Thank you. I came last year, but she made the night awful pointing out how I was alone. I know this isn't real, but I'm glad we met."

His lips parted as he smiled back. "I am too, but don't go getting ideas. I'm a good actor, but I make a terrible boyfriend."

CHAPTER 12

*a*va couldn't keep from looking at Justin as they finished dinner. It was like she was seeing through his facade for the first time. He claimed what he'd done with Tia was just him acting a role, but she didn't think so. It had felt genuine, and then he'd kept his arm around her even after they moved out of Tia's sight. Even now at the table, he had scooted his chair slightly so that though not touching, she could feel the heat from the proximity of his body. And he looked handsome in his tux. Most men did, but his tux appeared tailored perfectly for his body.

"So, what happens next?" he asked leaning closer to keep his voice quiet.

"A speaker will take the podium in a minute and they'll announce the winners for the different awards. Then there's usually dancing, but we don't have to stay for that part if you don't want." She offered him the out though she hoped he wouldn't take it. The thought of dancing close to him with his arms around her sent her heart racing.

"I suppose we could stay to dance." He looked around the room. "Will there be any photographers taking pictures? Dancing together would look great on a cover."

Ava shook her head unsure of the answer and even more unsure of everything else. Had she read more into his actions than existed? Maybe his nice guy act really was more for image than for her.

"Welcome everyone to the fifteenth annual Romance Gala. I'm Nancy Johnson, and I'm excited to be announcing the winners for our seven categories. As you know, all of these men and women work very hard throughout the year to put out the best romances possible. Some have many books out and some are brand new authors. We pride ourselves on finding the best talent out there. Without further ado, let's begin with our winner for the erotic romance genre." She held up a white envelope and waved it as if she were Vanna White indicating a new puzzle.

"Which category are you nominated for?" Justin whispered.

"Clean romance. I don't write erotica. Far from it."

"I should have guessed that," he said with a small smile before turning back to the presenter.

"The winner in our erotic genre is Devin Sheets."

Ava clapped along with the rest of the room as a woman with a large curly mane of dark hair took the stage.

"That's a pseudonym, right?" Justin sounded pained at the notion that might be her real name.

"Probably. Most erotic authors don't use their real names."

Devin Sheets gave her acceptance speech and then Nancy took the stage again. "Our historical romance is quite the large category. It covers everything up until about 1950, so the competition is quite fierce. This year, our winner is Bev Franklin."

Another round of clapping as an older woman with a head full of white hair took the stage.

"She looks like she's the historical fiction," Justin whispered.

Ava giggled and swatted his arm. "Be nice."

After Bev, they announced the contemporary romance award, the mystery and suspense award, and the paranormal romance award. The woman who won that resembled a wolf with her black and grey hair and stormy eyes.

"And our last romance category is our clean romance genre. This category has gained a lot of traction in the last year, so more competition filled the arena this year. The winner this year is Eleanor Katy."

Ava hadn't expected to win, but the disappointment stung nonetheless.

Justin placed a hand on her arm. "I'm sorry you didn't win."

"Me too, but Tia didn't either, so I count that as a win."

Justin's face scrunched in disgust. "She writes clean romance?"

Ava laughed and shushed him but it was nice to have someone in her corner this year even if it was just as a friend - or whatever Justin was.

"That brings us to our last category- our emerging author award. This is for a new author who shows promise. In order to qualify for this award, the author can have no more than two books out and they have to meet a sales and review quota. It is my pleasure to announce this year's winner is Ava McDermott."

Ava began clapping along with the rest of the crowd until it registered that Nancy had called her name. Her? She was the emerging author they'd chosen.

"Get up there." Something like admiration shone in Justin's eyes as he motioned for her to take the stage.

Ava pushed back her chair and stood. She plastered a smile across her face as she made her way to the front, but inside her wheels were turning ninety miles an hour. What was she going to say? She had no speech prepared. She hadn't even thought this was a possibility.

Nancy beamed as she handed over the golden pen award to Ava. With trembling hands, Ava took it and turned to the crowded room. She sought Justin among the sea of faces and his smile gave her the confidence to open her mouth.

"Wow, well, this was definitely unexpected, but I thank you. My first novel was really a gift from God, but I am so pleased. Now if I could just finish the next one." There was a titter of laughter from among the crowd. Most of them were authors and they had been there at one point in their career.

"Um, I'd like to thank Gen, my editor and friend. She's not here tonight, but she bleeds all over my initial drafts making them better than before. I know she edits for a few of you as well, so you know my pain." Another few chuckles reached her ears. "And my…" she faltered over the word boyfriend. It was what he was pretending to be and it would look awkward if she didn't say anything about him in the speech, but saying the word boyfriend out loud somehow made it more real. She couldn't do it. "Justin. I know we haven't been together long, but you inspire me with new ideas." Yes, that sounded plausible but not forced. "Thank you all again."

She held the award up to another round of cheering and clapping before stepping off the platform and making her way back to her seat. As she passed Tia's seat, she felt the evil glare of her eyes. The award was nice, but Ava wasn't sure it was worth giving Tia even more reason to hate her.

"Wow, I guess I should read this work of yours, you emerging author." Justin smiled at her as she sat back down.

"It's nothing, really." But that wasn't the truth. Getting recognized here was the first step into becoming truly successful, but it had also put a target on her back.

∾

*J*ustin couldn't believe he was having such a good time at this gala with Ava. It was weird how their differences didn't seem so pronounced here as they had in the cottage, and they felt even smaller as he twirled her around the floor.

"Mind if I cut in?" Justin turned to see Tia's fake smile radiating at him.

Ava stiffened in his arms, and he forced himself not to go off on this woman. She seemed intent on ruining Ava's night though he had no idea why. "I'm a little busy."

"Please, just one little dance." She placed a hand on his upper arm and batted her eyes. It probably worked on other men, but Justin had built up an immunity to women's charms, except, it seemed, for Ava's.

"Go on. I'll just get some punch and fresh air." Ava stepped out of his arms and motioned for Tia to take her place, but Justin didn't want to dance with Tia. He wanted to dance with Ava, but he was treading unknown water here. With no idea what past existed between these two women, he chose to take Ava's lead, and circled his arms around Tia but not before mouthing to Ava that he would come find her.

"So, you and Ava seem close. How long have you two been together?"

Justin narrowed his eyes at the blond. She was fishing for something. The only problem was he didn't know what. "A few weeks. What can I say? It was attraction at first sight." Which wasn't far from the truth. The image of her, wet and angry, attacking him still replayed often in his mind.

"Yes, well, attraction fades especially when you have nothing in common." She wrapped her arms around his neck forcing him to drop his to her waist and sway. "I did some research on you, Justin Miller, and I can't see that you two have much in common. Not like you and I would."

What was she getting at?

"See, I don't think you two are really a couple. I saw all the articles about you giving up on love, and then all of a sudden, out of the blue, you show up with Ava? I've been in the business long enough to know a PR repair job when I see one, but Ava is too vanilla for you. If you want a woman who can salvage your reputation and make it fun along the way, then I'd be happy to be that woman."

Ugh, was she for real? Justin had seen a lot of things in his ten years in Hollywood, but he still had trouble stomaching women like Tia. He dislodged her arms from around his neck and stepped back. "I think I'm done with this conversation, and I'd like to see where my date has gotten off to. Perhaps you should do the same."

Her eyes flashed fire as her lips pulled into a taut line. "Fine, but remember that I gave you an out. I won't be so nice in the future." With that, she whipped around, nearly swatting him across the face with her blond hair, and stalked away.

"What was that about?" Ava asked as she appeared beside him, a drink in each hand. She held one out for

Justin who took it and looked the direction Tia had disappeared.

"Your friend Tia is quite the piece of work."

Ava scoffed and wrinkled her nose. "She is no friend of mine."

"What's the beef between you two anyway?" He tipped back the cup and let the cool beverage coat his throat.

"We were friends a year ago. We met at a writer's conference and shared secrets about our books and the publishing process, but when my book had more success than hers, she turned on me claiming I had hired a ghostwriter. It's not that people don't do it, but she knew I hadn't. We had talked about how we wanted our writing to be our own."

"You should watch yourself around her. She hinted that she thinks our relationship is fake, and I wouldn't put it past her to try to out us."

"Thankfully I never see her except for events like this. We don't run in the same circles anymore."

While that might be true, Justin had known vindictive women before and he knew what they were capable of. He had a suspicion Tia was not all talk and no action.

He placed their empty cups on a nearby table and gathered Ava back into his arms, but the enjoyment of dancing with her was gone. Tia felt like an unknown, and Justin hated unknowns.

CHAPTER 13

"So, tell me all about the gala last night," Genevieve said as she lounged across Ava's bed.

Ava bit back a smile and ducked into her closet to grab the outfit she planned to wear tonight. She had been dying to tell Genevieve about it, but it had been too late when she'd made it back the night before. "It was nice. Tia Sweetchild was there."

"Ugh, I can't stand her."

Ava popped back out and held up the outfit to get Gen's approval. "Me either, but Justin totally put her in her place when she tried to rub it in that I didn't have a date last year. He amazed me."

Genevieve looked over the outfit, tilted her head, and narrowed her eyes at Ava. "Yeah, that's perfect. Amazed you, huh? And how about the rest of the night?"

"It was fine. They served delicious food. I won the emerging author award while Tia won nothing, so I consider that a win. We had several reporters approach us and take pictures which should be good for both of our images." Ava slipped out of her flannel pants and shirt and into the skirt and shirt she had brought out.

"Why do I feel like there's a 'but' coming?" Gen asked as she stretched out on the bed.

"Well, there was this weird moment where Tia cut in on our dancing, and Justin said she told him she knew the relationship was fake. He doesn't think it's anything to worry about, but he doesn't know Tia like I do."

"He's probably right. Tia won't come to our office, and even if she did you know I won't say anything. More than likely, she was just fishing for information."

"Maybe, but it still makes me nervous. What if it gets discovered? Won't that ruin my reputation as a writer?" Ava smoothed her skirt and regarded her reflection in the mirror.

"You worry too much. Even if it got discovered, it would be a flash in the pan story. People would forget about it quickly and move on. Your writing would be fine. Now, how about anything else? Like more practice on the kiss?" Gen wiggled her eyebrows suggestively.

Ava felt the heat sear across her face, and she averted her eyes. "This is a fake relationship, remember?" But the expression on Justin's face as he dropped her off flashed into her mind. She could have sworn there had been desire and struggle there as if he'd wanted to kiss her. And she'd wanted him to. At least she thought she had.

"Yeah, I remember. The question is, do you and Justin

remember? I watched his face when he couldn't take his eyes off you last night - like you were an ice-cold beer after a marathon."

"What? Who drinks beer after a marathon?"

Gen shrugged. "You know what I mean. And then he pulls this knight in shining armor routine? That doesn't sound like the man who hates romance you described." Genevieve crossed to the vanity and patted the seat for Ava to sit.

"I didn't say he was a knight in shining armor. It's not like he rescued me from a dragon, although describing Tia as a dragon isn't far off." She sat down and faced the mirror. "Besides, it's part of the game. He's pretending to care. Nothing more." Her eyes flicked to the mirror daring Gen to disagree, but Gen said nothing as she picked up the curling iron and began curling her hair. The silence forced Ava to ponder Gen's words. Justin had seemed different last night, but surely it had been her imagination. He had made it very clear he held no interest in a real romance and one night wouldn't change that. Would it?

She watched as Gen created cascading curls in her hair. It created an effect so different from her usual look. It wasn't that Ava couldn't curl her own hair; she simply rarely did. Maybe it was because she thought her time was better spent writing and maybe it was because she didn't want a man to fall in love with a perfect image only to find out she wore sweatpants and a ponytail around the house most days. She'd had a friend tell her stories of how she woke up at five am to put on makeup because she was terrified her husband would leave if he knew what she looked like without it. Ava didn't want a relationship like that. Better for him to see her flaws from the beginning.

The doorbell rang, jolting her mind back to the present. "That's Justin. Do I look okay?"

Genevieve flashed a knowing smile. "Yep. Good luck. Don't do anything stupid on national TV."

"Thanks for the boost of confidence." Ava stuck out her tongue at her friend before opening the door. "Don't forget to lock up when you leave," she hollered over her shoulder.

"Did I interrupt something?" Justin asked looking over her shoulder.

"No, just Gen being Gen." She pulled the door shut behind her and followed Justin to his car. "So, this is my first television interview. Is there anything I should know?"

"Yeah, avoid water. Trust me, the last thing you want to do is fight a full bladder on TV."

Ava chuckled as she pictured him squirming in his seat. "I take it you speak from experience?"

He shot her a pointed stare as he opened the car door. "It's not funny. The first time I appeared on a show, I was so nervous that I downed an entire bottle of water while I waited in the green room which had no bathroom. I thought it would be fine because I was supposed to go on twenty minutes later, but the guest in front of me had a seizure and they had to call an ambulance. Nearly an hour passed before they got her taken care of and came to get me. That left no time to use the bathroom as they were already behind in their filming. Needless to say, nerves combined with a full bladder do not make for a comfortable experience. It was the longest twenty minutes of my life."

"I wish I could have seen that." Ava couldn't help the smile that parted her lips as she slid into the seat. Justin rolled his eyes as he shut her door and walked around to his, but she had caught the ghost of a smile on his mouth.

The ride to the studio remained quiet, but not uncomfortable. Ava found it odd how they could sit in silence especially accounting for the fact they were still practically strangers. Though he didn't feel much like a stranger anymore.

She followed his lead when they pulled into the parking lot, and a surge of relief flooded her as he took her hand. Ava had no idea if that was part of the act, but gratitude filled her with the gesture.

He stopped outside the front door and turned to her. "Try not to be too nervous," he said squeezing her hand. "Remember, they smell fear."

Ava nodded and took a deep breath as he opened the door. A smart brunette manned the desk in the lobby and looked up at them as they entered.

"Hi, Justin Miller and Ava McDermott. We have an interview with Kevin Jones."

The brunette tapped a few keys on her computer. "Yes, sir. I'll call Vicky to come get you. It should just be a few minutes."

Vicky, a young woman with a headset glued to her ears

and a clipboard attached to her hands, showed up a few minutes later. She led them down the hallway to a small dressing room with a large mirror and two chairs. "Desi will be in shortly to check your makeup."

"Is she always so brusque?" Ava asked as she perched in one of the chairs.

Justin shrugged. "I don't recognize her from the last time I appeared, but it's not usually long from here. After they check makeup, they'll probably move us to the green room which leads to the stage when it's time."

A minute later another woman entered. Her blond hair was pulled into side pigtails but her clothes made the look appear hip instead of childish. "I'm Desi, and I'm here to make you beautiful. I know you think you are already, but believe me I work magic. What you've done doesn't always look good on HD, so please don't be offended if I change something." The smacking of her gum exaggerated the bored timbre of her voice, and Ava wondered how many times a day she gave the same spiel.

Desi motioned for Justin to sit first. She tilted his chin up and then side to side. "You must be in the industry," she said as she opened a container with powder. She dusted some across his forehead and the bridge of his nose and then stepped back.

"I'm a host for a dating show, and I've been doing my own makeup for TV for years." Justin's chest puffed out a little in pride and Ava mashed her lips together to keep from laughing. Only a TV personality would brag about his ability to put on makeup.

"I've been doing mine for years too," she said smiling up at Desi as she sat in the chair Justin had vacated. "Since the age of twelve anyway."

Desi tilted her head up and frowned. "Yeah? Well, there's a difference between doing your makeup and doing it for HDTV." She shook her head. "This eye color won't work."

Ava's smile faltered as Desi wiped a cool cotton ball across her lids. She couldn't believe she had to get her makeup redone while Justin's had been nearly perfect. He caught her eye and winked before dusting his shoulders as if congratulating himself. She stuck her tongue out at him. He could have at least warned her, so she hadn't opened her mouth like a complete fool. She'd had no idea doing your makeup for television was very different from everyday makeup. He grinned and stuck his tongue out at her in return, and Ava felt something in their relationship shift.

When Ava's makeup met Desi's satisfaction, she led them out of the room and to another area that Ava assumed must be the green room. Vicky, or headset girl as Ava had taken to calling her in her head, watched a screen that showed a live view of the stage. There were a few more chairs and no mirror in this room, but otherwise it appeared no different.

Justin sat in one of the chairs, but Ava paced in a small circle. She tugged on her shirt wishing suddenly that she had worn something different. This one felt too tight all of a sudden.

She glanced over at Justin, but he still appeared calm and collected. How could he not be nervous? There was no planning live television, and Justin liked to have everything planned out. Sure, Kevin Jones, the host, had given them questions he might ask, but Ava had heard stories about hosts deviating from those questions sometimes for whatever reason.

"Will you stop?" he asked as she tugged on her shirt again. "You're making me nervous, and I'm never nervous in front of the camera."

"Why shouldn't I be nervous?" she asked. "What if he asks us something we didn't practice?"

"Shh," he hissed in a low voice as he looked around. He crossed to her and placed his hands on her arms. Then he leaned down until his face was inches from hers. "We don't talk like that ever and especially not here. Look, I know this is new for you, but Kevin is generally a straight shooter. If it wasn't on the card, he probably won't ask it."

Ava swallowed as the nearness of him washed over her. His blue eyes stared into hers, and her breath caught. "Okay," she whispered breathlessly, "but you take the lead. You answer first and I'll chime in only if asked or add little details."

Her lips parted before she could stop them, and his gaze dropped to them before returning to her eyes. She could almost read the question of permission in his gaze, and she closed her eyes in assent.

"You guys are on in five," headset girl said from the

side of the stage and the moment shattered. Justin jumped away from her and reached for his tie.

Ava cleared her throat as she fought to bring her heartbeat back under control. "Can I get some water?" Suddenly, her throat was as dry as the Sahara Desert.

Headset girl rolled her eyes but a moment later a boy appeared with a water bottle in hand. Ava had just managed a sip when headset girl motioned them over.

"You're on."

Ava looked around for a place to put the water, but nothing was nearby and headset girl was ushering her out. Oh well, bringing a water bottle out wasn't that big of deal, right?

The sound of the applause hit her first and Ava froze as she scanned the room. It wasn't a large room, but it was packed. There were three sections with at least ten rows of ten chairs and a person filled each and every seat. She tried to do the math in her head. Was that three hundred people?

"Are you going to join us Ava?"

Ava looked to her left where Justin and Kevin were standing and staring her direction. "Oh, right, yes, sorry." She hurried to join them, her face hot, but as she did, her foot caught on something and she flew forward. Justin reached to catch her but her momentum carried her past his arms and into his chest. The water bottle squished between them, the force of their bodies popping the lid and sending water shooting into the air. Ava jumped back in surprise, but the damage was done. Water drenched her front sending her shirt clinging to her, but Justin's predicament was even worse. The water had landed on the crotch of his pants in a most unfortunate place.

A collective gasp erupted from the audience and Ava's hand flew to her mouth. "I am so sorry." Justin's gaze was unreadable as he wiped at his pants.

"Well, this is quite the way to make an entrance." Kevin took control of the situation, but he couldn't contain his smile either. "Ladies and gentlemen, Justin Miller and Ava McDermott. Why don't you guys have a seat and I'll have towels brought out."

The crowd laughed and cheered as headset girl ran out with two towels. Justin and Ava each took one and sat. As discreetly as possible, Ava patted her shirt hoping her pink bra wasn't showing underneath. She should have listened to Gen and wore the beige one, but she had claimed it was too boring. Well, it would definitely not be boring if her pink one was showing. At least Justin could hide his wet pants when seated. He folded the towel on his lap.

"So, Justin, you've been hosting 'Who Wants to Marry a Cowboy' for ten years, is that right?"

"That's right, Kevin. Ten years and going strong." Justin flashed his fake smile. He was way too good at that, and Ava wondered if she had even seen his real smile.

"Ten years is a long time to watch people fall in love especially when your life hasn't reflected that."

Justin's jaw tightened beside her, and Ava tried to contain her shock. This had not been on the list of questions, and it felt like Kevin hoped to anger Justin. She hoped he would keep his cool and answer the question because she certainly couldn't. His past relationships were an area Justin had refused to fill her in on. She knew his wife had died, but that had been as much as he'd shared.

"I've had my fair share of bumps but everyone has. Still," he picked up Ava's hand, and his smile stretched further, "love always wins in the end."

Ava forced a smile in return. He looked pained not happy, rather like the Joker from Batman.

"Yes, and we'll get to that in a second, but since you've been on the show, you've been married twice, is that right?"

Justin's grip tightened on Ava's hand. "Yes, that's right. My first wife passed away and a few years later I met my second wife."

"And she left you for her Botox doctor, is that right?"

The tension in the room lay heavy, tangible. Ava should say something, but what?

"She did." Veins bulged in Justin's throat and the muscles in his jaw tensed. Ava wasn't sure how much longer he would keep his cool.

"Her loss though." Ava's eyes widened when she realized she had said the words out loud and not in her head. "I mean if she hadn't, then I never would have met Justin."

Justin's eyes sent her a silent thank you as he squeezed her hand again. Kevin's eyes, however, roamed over her face as if searching for any sign of weakness.

"You're a romance writer, isn't that right Ava?"

She beamed, first at Justin and then at the audience. "I am. Love is important for what I do, and I think it is important for everyone to have in their life."

"Yet, you remained single up until recently as well, right?"

Kevin's words felt like an accusation, but Ava was determined to keep a calm demeanor. "That I was. I don't believe in falling in love with every man I date because I'm looking for something more serious."

Kevin's eyebrow lifted and he sat back. "And you found it with Justin? The man who claimed love was a fraud and relationships never last?" Disbelief was written all over Kevin's face.

Ava smiled at Justin. "I think we've all thought that at one time or another. Sometimes, when life throws you lemons, you get soured for a time before you realize you can use them to make lemonade."

"That is an interesting concept, and you certainly seem to have convinced Justin rather quickly. So, how exactly did you guys meet?"

Justin opened his mouth to answer, but Ava placed her free hand on his arm. She could tell Kevin was looking for any way to tear their story apart and she feared Justin would leave the romance out when he told it, leaving the door open for more questions.

"On the beach. Is there any place more romantic?" She smiled out at the audience earning some cheers. "I had booked a cottage to work on my next book and somehow they double booked Justin in the same cottage. We met on the beach as the sun was setting on the ocean and realized we had an attraction. The rest, as they say, is history." This time when she smiled out at the audience, she earned a chorus of ash.

~

*J*ustin smiled as he watched Ava spin their meeting. If she wrote anything like she told a story, then her books must be amazing. He was drawn in, and he knew it was false. Justin sneaked a glance at Kevin, but he too was mesmerized by Ava.

"I have to admit, it does sound like a good story, but we've received an anonymous tip that it's just that. A story, so what do you say to that?"

Justin's jaw clenched as the audience gasped and turned accusing eyes their direction. He'd been wrong to dismiss Tia. She was evidently more vindictive than he'd first thought. "I'd say you should vet your sources better, Kevin."

"And yet the timing is quite interesting. You just got back from Maui a few weeks ago, and your trip to the ocean seemed to coincide with your tainted image."

"You're right. My partner, Peter, thought I could use a break to re-center and remember why we started the show. He sent me to the cottage because he'd had a good experience there years before. He said magic happens there. I thought he was talking about my outlook," he turned and smiled at Ava, "but it turns out more than one kind of magic happens there."

That earned a chorus of 'ahs' from the audience and Justin knew he had turned the tide. Kevin wouldn't press anymore during this interview for fear of the crowd turning on him.

"Well, that definitely sounds sweet and goes to show that love can happen at any time. So, Ava, what's your next book going to be about?"

"Uh." A flush crawled across Ava's cheeks and her gaze shifted to the floor. "It's about a man who's given up on romance but meets his opposite and finds love again."

Kevin chuckled. "Write what you know? Am I right?"

Justin stared at Ava. He'd had no idea he was the topic of her new book, and curiosity coursed through him. How would she portray him? Would it be flattering? He supposed he better read it before he let her put it out there for the world to read.

"It does make it easier, but it's never all true. I take things that inspire me and then I put my own spin on them."

"Well, I'm sure we'll all look forward to reading it. And how about you, Justin? Do you have plans to continue with 'Who Wants to Marry a Cowboy' now that you've found love again?"

The question seemed innocent, but there was a gleam in Kevin's eyes that Justin didn't like. He would have to make sure he and Ava were seamless from here on out because he certainly wasn't sure they had convinced Kevin.

"I'm not sure what the future holds for me yet, Kevin, but 'Who Wants to Marry a Cowboy' has been my home, and it's always good to go home."

"And they're lucky to have you. Let's have another round of applause for Justin and Ava and true love."

Though the crowd cheered and Ava smiled, Justin's insides churned. That had been close, and he knew Kevin suspected their relationship was fake. The only question was if Kevin cared enough to pursue it. Justin wasn't a huge star, so Kevin might let it go, but then there was Tia. She'd gotten to Kevin quickly. Had she known of their appearance on the show or had she just shot off her knowledge to anyone who would listen?

"Well, that was interesting," Ava said as they left the studio.

Interesting? Not the word he would have chosen to describe it. Disastrous was a little closer. He thought they'd managed to salvage it, but how well would be determined by the spin in the papers tomorrow. "It was not as good as I'd hoped, but you did great. You are quite the story teller."

"But?"

"But I was watching Kevin, and I don't think he bought it entirely. Plus, I'm fairly certain Tia was his source. We just have to be careful. Make sure every "T" is crossed and every "I" is-" The ringing of his cell phone interrupted his statement. "Hang on."

Surprise and dread filled Justin as he recognized Elizabeth's number on the screen. He frowned but punched the button. "Hello?"

"Justin? It's Liz. Hear me out before you say no. Garrett called me this morning, and he's sick."

Justin scoffed. "Yeah, I've known that for years."

"No, I mean health-wise. His leukemia has gotten worse and he needs a bone marrow transplant."

Justin was already shaking his head. "Liz, no. You can't ask me to do that. Hasn't he taken enough from me?"

"He's tried to apologize to you for over a year, Justin, but you haven't let him."

"And I'm not about to start now. Listen, I'm sorry he's sick, but he needs to look elsewhere." Justin hung up the phone without saying goodbye, but he'd forgotten Ava was right there. She fixed a questioning gaze on him.

"Is everything okay?"

"Yeah, that was my sister. My half-brother is sick and needs a bone marrow transplant. She wants me to get tested."

"But you don't want to?" Her words were slow and hesitant as if she didn't understand his unwillingness. And why would she? He hadn't even told her about his half-brother, much less the whole story.

Justin sighed and ran a hand across his chin. "My brother is a plastic surgeon." He let the words sit there knowing they would make sense to her in a minute. At least if she had been paying attention.

"I don't understand," she said with a shake of her head.

"Specifically, a Botox doctor."

Her brow furrowed for a moment as she looked at him

and then her eyes widened. He knew the light switch had been flipped. "Not the same Botox doctor that stole your second wife?"

"The very one. How's that for irony?"

Ava placed a hand on his arm and turned a soft gaze on him. "Maybe he's changed. We all make mistakes."

Justin shook her hand off. "Not Garrett. He's always been like this. We haven't spoken in years, and I'm not about to give him anything much less bone marrow from my body."

"But he's your brother-"

"Half-brother and he was, but he isn't any more." Justin felt the anger boiling up. He'd tried so hard to not think about Garrett and Candy, and Liz had destroyed it all in one night with her phone call. He closed his eyes and took a deep breath to calm the fire within. This wasn't Ava's fault, and he shouldn't take it out on her. "Come on, I'll take you home."

CHAPTER 14

*A*va leaned against the brown Formica counter and stared into her empty mug as her thoughts swirled around in her head.

"Oh, there you are. I thought you were just getting a drink, but when you didn't come back for ten minutes, I began to wonder." Genevieve stood in the doorway of the little office kitchen. It wasn't really much of a kitchen, but as it contained a small fridge, an even smaller stove top, and two cabinets that held plates and silverware, Ava classified it as a kitchen. It didn't, however, have the room for a table and chairs which was why she leaned against the counter currently.

She pointed to the simple black kettle next to her that sat on the stovetop. "It hasn't whistled yet." In fact, it took ages for the burner to heat up the kettle. Ava probably could have walked to the nearby coffee shop and ordered a tea faster than her water would heat up, but she hadn't wanted to. She wasn't even sure she wanted tea as much as she wanted the quiet stillness waiting for the water to boil brought. Her computer wasn't in here mocking her, and so she could let her mind wander to the thoughts that consumed it anyway.

Genevieve's brow arched slightly and she crossed her arms as she leaned into the doorframe. "Uh huh. Well, you guys looked good on the show last night. Very believable."

Ava nodded but her mind wasn't on the show. It was still firmly fixated on the conversation she'd had with Justin after the show. The one where he turned his back on his estranged brother, and of course how she could fix it.

Ava understood sibling rivalry. Her sister had been the pretty one - the one who always won prom queen and homecoming queen and pickle queen - a crown title reserved for girls who lived in Piedmont, her hometown - though Ava wasn't sure Kelsie had been quite as excited about that one. And her brother, Tristan? He'd been the brains of the family. The one who'd attended medical school and now headed the trauma unit at one of the biggest hospitals in the state. And she'd been the dreamer. The one who escaped into books and writing. The one who created characters and plots who found their happily ever afters because she couldn't seem to find hers in real life. But even though she and her siblings were different, she'd never turn her back on them if they needed bone marrow. Of course, they hadn't stolen her husband either, not that she had one. Still, she needed to find a way to get Justin to give his brother a chance to apologize.

"Uh oh, I know that look. What's going on?" Genevieve crossed to the cupboard and retrieved a mug for herself, but she didn't wait for the piercing whistle of the kettle. She turned instead to the Keurig machine and popped a pod in. "You know this makes tea too and it's faster than your kettle method," she said as the machine began its familiar warm up groans and gruntings.

Ava shrugged. "It's not the same." The kettle elicited its shrill cry at that moment and she turned the burner off, dropped a tea bag in the mug, and poured in the water. Then she picked up the mug and cradled it in her hands, enjoying the warmth emanating from the ceramic sides. "It's Justin. He got a call from his sister last night. It seems his brother needs a bone marrow transplant and wants to know if he's compatible, but he refuses to even get tested."

"What?" Gen picked up her mug, blew lightly on the brew, and then braved a sip. "Why?"

Ava sighed and shook her head. "Evidently his brother is the Botox doctor his second wife ran off with."

Genevieve let out a low whistle. "Whoa, that's pretty heavy."

"Yeah," Ava bit the inside of her lip and watched the amber liquid swirl in her cup. "They haven't spoken in years, but I feel like they need to. Like maybe forgiving his brother will help Justin move past his anger and his hatred of romance."

Gen's eyebrow arched. "Are you hoping they'll reconnect for his sake or for yours?"

"What?" Ava pushed herself off the counter and

headed back toward the main office, making sure to keep her eyes on her drink and away from Genevieve's prying gaze. "I don't know what you're talking about."

"Oh, yes you do. You're developing feelings for this guy, aren't you?"

Ava set her mug down at her scratched and scarred desk. It had been a hand-me-down from her father when he upgraded his office equipment, but Ava loved it. She held fond memories of writing at this desk while her father spoke with clients in the other room. Her initials were still engraved on the side though he had been peeved the day she had done that.

She pulled out the ergonomic chair - *that* she had splurged on - and sat down. "No, of course not. It would never work out. He doesn't even attend church, and you know a relationship with God is important to me." Ava glanced up but Genevieve had her head cocked in the 'uh huh, I don't believe you' expression that she used whenever she thought Ava was lying.

"And if he did?"

Ava sighed. "Okay, I don't know. I mean I know I shouldn't be attracted to him for all the reasons I just gave, but..." Ava shrugged as she let the statement trail off. She had spent last night dissecting the dilemma. She wanted to believe her desire to help Justin was altruistic and had nothing to do with her, but the truth was she did feel something for him. She just wasn't sure if it was friendship or something more.

Genevieve sat down at her desk across the room. "Well,

I think you better figure that out before you go in trying to Dr. Phil things you may not understand."

Ava's breath exited in a small sigh as she turned back to her screen. Gen was right of course. She was the more rational one. Ava tended to leap first and ask questions later, and on more than one occasion, that had landed her in hot water. Still, she couldn't shake the feeling she was supposed to do something especially after the weird way they met in the first place.

~

*J*ustin punched the ignore button and pocketed his cell phone as he stepped into the office he and Peter shared. Garrett had been calling all morning, but Justin had nothing to say to him. Not now. Not ever.

Peter looked up from his computer as Justin entered. "I watched the show last night. She's good."

Justin sat down and punched the button to turn his laptop on. A tiny hum filled the room and the screen blinked to life. "Yeah, she is, but that was just one show, and Kevin wasn't entirely convinced. It's going to take more than that to turn the image around."

"It may not take as long as you think. Check the headlines."

Justin pulled up a browser and clicked into the URL bar. He typed The Evening Show and hit enter. The screen blanked and then a picture of Ava and him smiling at the camera filled the screen. Underneath was a short article with a bold heading. "Has the Grinch found his mate?" he read aloud. His eyes flicked to Peter's. "I'm not sure that's exactly helping my image. They're still calling me The Grinch."

"They are," Peter said with a wave of his hand, "but they're talking about the two of you. And they're not the only ones. The article ran on Star Weekly and Hollywood Today."

"That's good." Justin's attention returned to his computer screen. He had loaded his email and now stared at one from Garrett. Did he read it? Delete it?

"Good, huh? What's going on with you?"

Justin looked up, sighed, and raked his hand across his chin. The stubble scraped like sandpaper across the palm of his hand. He didn't normally skip shaving but last night he'd lain awake so long thinking about Candy and Garrett and Ava that he'd slept through his alarm - another thing he rarely did. "Liz called last night."

"Uh oh."

Justin nodded. He'd known Peter long enough that Peter knew his background and that a call from his sister rarely proved a good thing. The relationship between his sister and him remained tentative at best. "Yeah, evidently Garrett is sick and needs a bone marrow treatment. They want me to get tested."

Peter's chair groaned as he leaned back in it. They both agreed it was time for new furniture, but neither of them had made the first move to look for any more. Justin no longer knew if it was because neither of them liked shopping or if they both held a fondness for the furniture that had been with them since the beginning of the journey.

"And what do you want?"

Now that was the question of the day. What did he want? He wanted to pretend Garrett didn't exist, but he couldn't really do that. Even though they were only half brothers, they were still brothers. It was one thing to ignore him but it was another thing entirely to let his brother die. Justin didn't even know if they were a match, but could he live with himself if they were and he did nothing to help?

After all, he'd grown up taking care of Garrett. Justin had been six when his parents divorced, and he'd been eight when Garrett was born. Though the age difference was significant, Justin had always wanted a brother, and he'd let Garrett join him in all the neighborhood games. It had been Justin, not his mother, who cleaned up Garrett's first skinned knee when he fell off his bike, and it had been Justin who iced his eye the time Garrett tried to catch a fly ball with his face.

And honestly, the whole Candy thing wasn't even completely Garrett's fault. Justin had fallen prey to her charms as well, so he knew how convincing she could be. And Candy had been much younger than Justin. In fact, she was just a year older than Garrett. They'd probably had more in common. It didn't make what he did okay - Garrett should have put his foot down and turned away Candy's advances - but he hadn't. Still, though Justin didn't agree with what happened, he could see how it happened.

"I don't know. Ava says I should give him a chance to explain, but I don't know if I want to hear it."

Another loud squeak filled the air as Peter leaned forward. "You told Ava?"

"She was with me when Liz called. I couldn't very well not tell her." But Justin knew what Peter was thinking. He had dated few people after Candy and none of them knew about Garrett. That subject was off limits even to Peter most of the time.

"Are you falling for this girl?"

It was a simple question and one Justin should have been able to answer no to quickly, but the truth was that he wasn't sure. The last two weeks had been a roller coaster of emotions and his insides felt like they had been ripped out through his stomach and shoved back in through his mouth. Yet Ava had been there with him through all of it, and he liked the thought of her being around. And that thought scared him.

"No," he lied, "this is just business." He cringed as he thought back to his harsh words to her the previous night. "Besides, she's way too different from me - a believer." He shook his head. "It would never work long term. Honestly, I'm surprised people are buying this relationship now."

"If I remember correctly, you were a believer once."

"Yeah, once. Before God took Carol and then decided to twist the knife in further with Candy and Garrett. He's probably enjoying watching this predicament unfold."

"Somehow I doubt that," Peter said. He looked as if he wanted to push the issue further, but they'd had this discussion before. "Anyway, finding love again wouldn't be the worst thing in the world."

But it would be because in order to find love, he would have to open his heart again, and every time he had done that, it had been torn apart. No, he needed to take these feelings for Ava, whatever they were, and forget them. She was a means to an end, a new career, and that was it.

CHAPTER 15

*A*va stared at the screen and ran a slender hand across her chin. Why was this book proving so challenging? Was it the looming deadline? The fear that her last book's success had been a fluke and she wasn't really talented? Or was it Justin? She'd thought of little else all day though she still hadn't thought of a way to help him and his brother.

Her phone vibrated beside the computer and she picked it up sighing as her mother's name flashed across the screen. Of course her mother would be calling, she had probably seen or heard about Ava's appearance on The Evening Show and was calling to find out who the new man was and why Ava hadn't told her about him. Could she ignore it? She hadn't practiced her words yet, and she hated lying to her mother.

With a sigh, Ava punched the button and mentally

prepared herself for the onslaught of questions. "Hey mom."

"Hey yourself. When were you going to tell me you had a new boyfriend? I had to find out from Elaine who saw you on tv."

Elaine was her mother's best friend and an avid tv watcher. Even when Ava had lived at home, she would often come over and regale them with information about the newest show on TV. She spoke of the characters like they were her friends, and Ava often wondered if she did anything else when she was home.

"I'm sorry Mom, but we just started dating." Ava had no intention of bringing Justin to meet her parents. One, they would never approve once they found out his feelings about God, and two, they would probably see through the facade and then get on her case for ever taking the deal in the first place. She was even beginning to wonder if the delusion remained beneficial. Her book still lay unfinished, her mind still refused to cooperate, and the ride back to her house last night had been stilted and stiff, almost like the first day they met.

"So, you'll tell the whole world on national television, but you won't tell your mother?"

Ava rolled her eyes and spun away from the computer screen. No way she could concentrate on the words with her mother's voice in her ear. "He's a tv show host, Mother. People wanted an interview with him when they found out about us."

"Well, can't you tell me anything about him?"

"His name is Justin Miller and he hosts a reality dating show."

A knock sounded at her door, and she crossed the room. She had no idea who would be showing up on her doorstep at this time, but the distraction was welcome. She peeked through the spy hole and bit her lip.

"Is that all you can tell me? Are you sure you two are even dating?"

"Mom, I have to go. Justin's here. Call you later." Without waiting for her mother to respond, Ava punched the end call button. She would deal with her mother later, when she had more to tell her and had the story more practiced.

She opened the door and leaned against the frame. "I wasn't expecting to see you again so soon."

"Good. I wanted to surprise you. I got reservations for Genaro's tonight." His eyes scanned her face. "I'm not interrupting anything am I?"

Ava sighed. "No, I was trying to write but not succeeding."

Justin's eyes flicked over her shoulder as if making sure he really wasn't keeping her from something important. "Well maybe this will help. Get some food to power that creativity."

"Sure, it's not like I'm getting any work done here." Ava grabbed a jacket before locking the door and following Justin to his car.

As she pulled her seatbelt across her chest, Ava glanced over at Justin. He looked a little different today, but she couldn't place her finger on what. His jeans still sported the perfect pleat and his shirt was nicely pressed too. Her eyes traveled upward and she gasped. His hair. It looked... not perfect.

"What?" He asked as he caught her staring at him.

"You looked more relaxed and I was trying to figure out why. It's your hair. It's not perfect."

"Uh, thank you?"

Ava laughed. "Sorry, that didn't come out the way it sounded in my head. It's a compliment, and it looks good. It's nice to see you relax a little."

He flashed her a small smile. "Maybe you're rubbing off on me."

Was he flirting with her? Or was this still part of the act? He was so hard to read sometimes. Every time she thought she had him figured out, he would do or say something to contradict her thinking.

As the silence settled in the car, her mind drifted from his possible flirtation to his definite problem. Had he talked to his brother? Should she broach the subject with him? She wanted to help, but he had seemed so resistant last time. "Anything new in your world?" Ava tried to sound nonchalant, but he could probably see right through her.

He glanced away from the steering wheel long enough to fix her with a pointed stare. "I'm not calling Garrett if that's what you are referring to."

"I understand he wronged you, but he was your brother long before your ex-wife came into the picture."

Justin shook his head and rolled his eyes. "No offense,

but seeing as how you've never been married, I'm not sure you're the person to be doling out advice."

Ava blinked at his harsh words. "Just because I haven't been married doesn't mean I don't know about betrayal." Her gaze fell to her lap. "I was engaged once."

Justin shot another glance her direction but no venom existed in this one. "You were? What happened?"

"College," Ava said with a shrug. "I thought we would end up together, but he was a year ahead of me in college, so he graduated first. He threw himself into his work and decided it was more important than me and called off the wedding."

"I'm sorry, but it was his loss. If he could see you now, I doubt he would sing the same tune."

Ava wasn't sure of the truth in that, but there was no sense ruining the date by arguing with him.

When they arrived at the restaurant, the hostess whisked them back to a secluded booth. She stayed just a little too long shooting longing glances at Justin under lowered lids that he seemed not to notice. Or perhaps he was so used to them that he just ignored them. Ava wondered if this happened often.

Unable to elicit a response from Justin, the hostess finally slinked away and Ava picked up the menu. "Everything looks delicious," she said as she scanned the offerings.

"Italian is my favorite kind of food though I don't eat it often," Justin replied. His menu lay unopened in front of him. Either he wasn't eating, or he had the menu so memorized that he knew what he wanted without looking.

Well, that was one more thing they had in common. Italian was her favorite food too. Too bad that brought the grand total of their commonalities to about three. Still, pretending to date him wasn't as bad as she'd thought it would be. True, they had only been on three dates so far counting this one, but they had all been.... nice. In fact, they had been nicer than the last few dates she had been on with men she had more in common with. Could there be something to that opposites attract saying?

"So, how is the image remake going?" She glanced up at him from the corner of her eye to gage his reaction.

The corners of his lips twitched. "It's going well. You impressed Peter with your performance on The Evening Show, and while we still need to be careful, the first responses have been favorable. Another solid few weeks and some more exposure might be enough to turn the tide in my favor."

"That soon, huh?" The thought of just another few weeks hit her hard. She shouldn't care. It wasn't like they would end up together, but a few weeks seemed too short. "I thought you said a month or two."

His brow lifted as he gazed at her. "I did, but I didn't know how much of a natural you would be. How about you? How are book sales going?"

"I don't really know," Ava said. "I don't see the results for three months, but I've definitely seen a rise of engagement on my author page."

"That's great news. Oh, hang on." His face clouded slightly as he pulled out his cell phone. He swiped the screen and his frustration faded to a look of confusion.

"What is it?" It was none of her business but watching his face was like watching a game of charades and not being able to guess. She picked up her water glass and took a sip.

"It's a friend request. I don't get them often. I only set up the page because the show's publicist said I needed to. It's from someone named Selene McDermott. Do you know her?"

Ava coughed, nearly spewing out the water she had just swallowed and her wild eyes met his gaze. It couldn't be. She grabbed for the phone in his hands. "Let me see that." She turned the screen to her and groaned even as a flame of embarrassment licked up her neck. "That is my mother. She called just before you picked me up asking about you. I had no idea she would stalk you, but I'm sure the friend request was an accident."

Justin chuckled as he took back his phone. "You must be close to her."

"We are. My whole family is close even though I'm the only one who still lives close. My sister is a model and my brother is a surgeon."

Justin dropped his gaze to the table. "It must be nice."

The waitress appeared at their table interrupting Ava's response. "Do you two know what you'd like?"

"I'll have the Chicken Alfredo," Ava said.

Justin smiled at her before placing an order for the same thing.

When the waitress left, Ava turned back to their previous conversation. "So, your family isn't close? I mean I know you and your brother aren't, but the rest of your family?"

Justin picked up a slice of bread from the basket in the middle of the table and turned it in his hand. "We used to be once. I remember some good times before my father left, but then it was just my mom, Elizabeth, and me. Those were tough times. Then they got better again when she married Ryan, my stepfather, and they had Garrett. Even though we were eight years apart, we were thick as thieves growing up. But then," he shrugged, "Candy happened and we weren't so close anymore. My mother and Elizabeth didn't want to take sides which felt like they were taking sides. At least to me."

Ava wished she had the right words to say to him "You know you could mend things with your brother. It might bring your family closer together."

"I'm not sure there is anything left worth mending," Justin said. Then he took a bite of his bread and Ava knew the discussion was over. At least for now. She would just have to keep praying that God would work on Justin's heart.

∾

*J*ustin watched Ava as her fork sliced through her cheesecake. She had surprised him by ordering it after completely cleaning her plate at dinner as well. Unlike most of the women Justin knew after living and working in Hollywood for the last decade, Ava appeared to have a healthy appetite, and he found it refreshing. In fact, he found a lot of things refreshing about her.

The waitress quietly dropped off the bill as Ava finished her dessert. Justin opened the black folder and scanned the itemized list before pulling a hundred-dollar bill from his wallet.

"I could help with that," Ava offered.

"No, my treat, remember? So, how is the new book going?" He slid the bill behind the receipt and closed the folder. The waitress would get a nice tip tonight.

"It's going okay. Not quite as good as I'd hoped."

"Why not? What's the issue? I thought you had a debonair character you were basing it on." He grinned and brushed his shoulders in a showing off motion.

She flashed a small smile at him before sighing. "Genevieve says it's because I'm not experiencing life."

"What do you mean?"

Another tinge of color flashed across her cheeks. "I'm a romance writer, but this is my first date in months. Gen thinks I need to date more and do something daring so I can give my stories a spark."

Daring? Hmm, well he doubted any truly daring place

would be open this late, but there was a band that played in a gazebo just a block away, and on clear nights like this, there would usually be couples dancing in the street. Perhaps that would be daring enough for her. "Well, maybe we can do something about that." He stood and held out his hand to her.

Her eyes narrowed as she took his hand. "How?"

He shook his head and smiled mischievously. "Not telling. You'll have to trust me."

"Trust you? Your idea of romance was a hot dog stand, remember? I'm not sure I should trust your idea of daring."

"Actually," he said with a laugh, "you said hot dog stand. I just said it didn't matter where we ate."

She smiled and rolled her eyes as they exited the restaurant. "Okay, fine, but I still don't know if I should trust you."

But he could tell she did. There was no hesitation as she let him pull her down the street and toward the music. Her eyes widened as she realized what he'd had planned. "Someone interrupted our dancing the last time, so I thought we could continue here. Besides, dancing in the streets isn't something you can do every day."

"You're right about that. I've never danced in the street before."

As her arms wrapped around his neck and his circled her waist, Justin felt himself fall. He'd been denying his feelings since the day they'd kissed, but he didn't want to run from them any longer. She turned her beautiful face up to him, her lips wide with her smile, and he couldn't stop himself. His face lowered to taste her lips again, and she did not pull away.

"Maybe we could make this relationship last a little longer," he said brushing his finger across her lips as he pulled back.

"I'd like that," she breathed.

He kissed her again, but when he pulled back this time, something caught his eye. Some movement off to the side. He turned his attention from her and scoured the crowd. Someone had been watching them. Someone blond. He was almost sure of it, but the only faces he saw now were the happy faces of the other couples around them.

"What's wrong?" she asked sensing his change.

"I thought I saw someone watching us, but there's nothing there now. Probably just someone enjoying the show." He smiled at her to assure her, but he wasn't convinced of that. He would have to pay more attention to his surroundings from now on.

CHAPTER 16

*A*va stood outside the office of Garrett Miller, plastic surgeon, as she debated if this was what she should be doing. Justin had been pretty clear he wanted nothing to do with Garrett, but Ava knew he would never forgive himself if something happened to him.

She'd had a friend die in college from alcohol poisoning and even though Ava hadn't given her friend the drinks, she'd lived with the guilt of thinking she could have saved her. It had been right before finals week and Ava stayed home to study. The next afternoon, she'd stopped by her friend's dorm to apologize, but she hadn't even gotten close to her room. Yellow caution tape sealed off the room, and a crowd of people filled the hallway and passed back the rumor she'd been found dead that morning.

No, she couldn't let that happen to Justin. She had to at

least try to help. With fresh resolve, she pushed open the door and stepped inside.

"Can I help you?" the receptionist asked. A vision of perfection, Ava wondered if she were a client as well as an employee.

"I was hoping to speak with Dr. Miller."

"Are you a patient?" the woman asked looking her over with discerning eyes.

Ava tried to keep her voice from shaking as she shook her head. She was way out of her element here. "No, I'm a friend of his brother's. Please, will you tell him I'm here about Justin?"

The woman cocked an eyebrow but reached for the phone. "Dr. Miller, there's a woman here who says she's a friend of your brother's." She paused for a minute and glanced back at Ava. "Very well. I'll tell her. He said to take a seat and he'll be with you in a moment," the woman said as she replaced the phone.

Ava sat and ran her hands down her thighs. She'd planned what she would say on the way over here, but now that she was here, all of her words sounded silly.

A moment later, a door opened and a man emerged. She would have guessed he was Garrett even if he hadn't looked pale and thin. Though his hair was dark, he shared the same ocean blue eyes that Justin did along with the distinguishing cleft in his chin.

"I'm Garrett Miller. What can I do for you?"

Ava stood and crossed to him. "I'm Ava McDermott.

I'm a friend of your brother's and I was hoping that maybe I could do something for you. Can we talk?"

He regarded her with an intrigued expression before turning to the receptionist. "Diane, hold my calls for half an hour."

"Yes sir," the woman said.

Ava breathed a sigh of relief as Garrett led the way down the hall to an office. "I'm sorry to just show up like this, but I've just recently starting dating Justin, and I understand you need a bone marrow transplant and Justin is refusing to get tested. I also know he'll regret it if he doesn't, and I'm hoping we can come up with a way to get him to change his mind."

"That's a nice thought," Garrett said as he sat down behind the desk, "but he isn't returning my phone calls. Hasn't for a year now. I can't say that I blame him, but I'd like to apologize and tell him that for whatever it's worth, he was right about Candy."

Ava took the chair he motioned to and leaned forward. "What do you mean?"

Garrett chuckled. "He told me Candy was bad news - that he'd been seeing signs of it before she left him - but I was stubborn. Justin had always been my idol and here was this beautiful woman who finally wanted me over him. It was wrong, and I guess deep down I knew it would ruin our relationship but I did it anyway. For about a year everything was great, but when I got sick, Candy showed her true colors. Said she couldn't be a nursemaid and left. I realized then what an awful mistake I'd made and tried to apologize to Justin, but it was too late."

"So, he's not aware you're no longer together?"

Garrett shrugged. "I doubt it. He never heard it from me and he and Liz aren't that close either. Plus, she's told me he never lets her talk about me. Why? Do you think it will make a difference?"

"I have no idea," Ava said with a shake of her head, "but I'd like to at least try. This might sound insensitive, but how long do you have if you don't get the transplant?"

"Six months, maybe a year, but I can feel it this time, so I think it will be faster."

Ava's heart broke for him. "Would you mind if I prayed for you?"

Garrett's eyes narrowed. "Justin's dating a believer? Never thought that day would come again after Carol's death."

"I'm still working on him too," Ava said, "but I have hope he'll come back to God."

"Well, I'm not much of a believer myself, but I'll take help wherever I can get it."

Ava reached across the desk and took hold of Garrett's hand. "Lord, I don't know Garrett well, but I sense his sincerity, and I recognize that you are about reconciliation. Please give us the wisdom to make that reconciliation happen, and Lord, please place your healing touch on Garrett. Heal his body and renew his spirit and help him to see you. Amen."

"Thank you," Garrett said. "No one's prayed for me in a long time." He stood and motioned her to do the same. "I'm not sure it will do any good, but I'm glad you stopped by."

"Me too."

⁓

*J*ustin couldn't help but whistle as he entered the office. He'd been riding high all day after that kiss with Ava last night, and he didn't care who knew it. But his whistle faded as he caught sight of Peter's face. "What's wrong?"

"You haven't been online, have you?" Peter asked.

"No, I worked out this morning and then showered. I haven't had a chance to watch anything or check out any social media. Why?"

Peter shook his head. "I don't think you're going to like it."

He turned his screen around and Justin's blood ran cold. Under the headline 'Betrayed Again' was a picture of Ava outside Garrett's office and then another one of them in the office. It was obviously taken with a long-range lens from outside as it wasn't super clear, but Justin made out Ava's hand on Garrett's arm. "Seriously? This cannot be happening again."

"Maybe it's not what you think," Peter said. "Is there another reason she might be there?"

"Who cares why she's there? I told her I didn't want anything to do with Garrett and she went anyway. Then she made me a fool by getting caught on film. How bad do you think the damage will be?"

"Well, that depends on you. You have the opportunity to take the high road here, Justin. As long as you don't go off spouting how angry you are and how you hate love, then you could actually garner sympathy. Right now, most of the vitriol is pointed at Ava."

"Good. I can't believe I let myself fall again. I should never have let you talk me in to this fake relationship."

Peter opened his mouth to speak, but Justin was done listening. He needed to walk and let off some steam. Without saying goodbye, he stormed out of the office. At least the show was not in session, so he had the lay of the compound mostly to himself.

Justin could not wrap his mind around the idea of Ava betraying him. Everything had been going so well last night, and then this. Why had he opened his heart again when relationships only seemed to destroy it? But if he were honest, the answer to that question was clear. It was because he had glimpsed a life with Ava and liked it. He had tasted how happy he could be again, and with one move she had destroyed it.

As he reached the front of the office again, an overwhelming urge to confront her welled up within him. He unlocked his car and climbed in taking a deep breath to calm his anger slightly before taking off. As angry as he was, he recognized driving emotionally was not a good idea.

Ava opened the door with a smile that froze when she saw him. "What's wrong?" she asked.

"How could you, Ava? I told you Garrett had betrayed me in the worst way and you went to him?"

Her face clouded with confusion. "How did you know I went to see him?"

Justin yanked out his phone and pulled up one of the articles. "Everyone knows, Ava. Someone caught you on film. Tia probably."

Her hand flew to her mouth as she scanned the article. "Justin, I'm so sorry. I thought I was helping."

"Some help," he said with a sneer. "Now I'm the piteous host whom women leave."

"Justin, I wasn't leaving you. Do you want to come inside and talk about this?" Her phone buzzed and she flipped it over glancing quickly at the screen.

"No, I don't want to talk about it. I'm obviously keeping you from something more important anyway. Probably my brother calling."

Her face flared with anger. "Stop that. You know I'm not interested in your brother. I was hoping to save you from the guilt I feel every day. You see, I had a friend die in college and I've always felt I could have saved her. I didn't want the same thing happening to you, and I thought if I could talk to Garrett, maybe there would be a way to reach you."

He opened his mouth to tell her to mind her own business, but before he could respond, her phone buzzed again. She glanced down again, but this time her eyes widened, and her hand flew to her mouth. "Oh no."

"What is it?" Something was wrong. It was etched in every worry line on her face, and as angry as he was with her, he was also concerned.

"It's my mom. She said my dad had a heart attack. He's on the way to the hospital. I have to go." She ducked back in the apartment and began frantically searching for something. "Keys? Where are my keys?"

"How about I drive you there?" The words were out before he had time to think them through or ponder the ramifications. He was still mad at her. Her family would be there. Was he ready to meet her family? Especially under circumstances like this? And it was a hospital. He hadn't been in one since Carol died. Could he step foot in one again?

Ava shook her head. "You don't have to do that. You're angry with me right now, and you don't even know my father."

Her tone triggered something inside him, and he realized right then he would go with her. She sounded scared and he wanted to be there for her. "You're right. I don't know your father and I am angry with you, but I can see you are hurting. Besides, I don't think you should drive in your condition."

He held up her hand which was shaking ever so slightly. Maybe it wouldn't be bad enough to hinder her driving and maybe it would stop if she got behind the wheel, but he didn't want to take that chance. As angry as he was with her, he didn't want her getting in an accident.

Her eyes focused on her hand and then met his gaze. "Okay, you're right."

CHAPTER 17

*J*ustin glanced over at Ava as he pulled into the hospital parking lot. She still lay curled inside herself as she had been for the whole drive. Her face never left the window though the blank gaze of her eyes left him wondering if she had seen anything.

He understood though. He remembered how he had been when Carol was dying. The same blank stare that coated her gaze filled his eyes then which brought up his current conundrum. Should he go in with her? Anger still burned inside him, but he wanted to be supportive for her.

Could he even go in with her? Just being in the parking lot of a hospital, even a different one than where Carol died, had dried his mouth up. His pulse beat faster than normal pounding like a drum in his ears. Would he even be able to make it inside and be her strength?

"Hey, we're here." He turned off the engine and touched her arm. She jumped as if his touch was fire instead of fingers. The vacant look in her eyes stirred his heart.

"What if he dies?" Her voice was barely more than a whisper, but it didn't need to be louder. Those four little words held all the weight in the world.

"He's not going to die." Justin couldn't know that for sure, but he needed it to be true. Ava appeared closer to her father than he was to his own. He'd never met the man, but it seemed obvious that losing him would deal a massive blow to Ava.

"Okay." She sniffed and ran a finger under each eye. No tear escaped, but perhaps it was a preemptive swipe. "Will you come in with me?"

And there it was. He wouldn't say no. Couldn't say no, but in agreeing, he was stepping on the boundary lines of this fake relationship. He could feel it shifting, almost like a chasm created during an earthquake. If he went with Ava, he suspected that the foundations of that carefully constructed wall would crumble into dust. He'd have to put his anger aside and there might be no turning back after this moment.

"Of course I will." Now he hoped his body would agree. He closed his eyes and took a deep breath as his therapist taught him years ago when the pain of losing Carol grew too great. When his pulse slowed, he stepped out of the car, walked around to Ava's side, and helped her out.

She grasped his hand tightly as they walked up the

sidewalk as if he were a lifeline tethering her to reality. She appeared small and frail next to him.

Justin tried to keep his breathing slow and regular, but he could feel the weight on his shoulders with every step they took, and he forced himself not to shiver. He hated hospitals. Even before Carol's death he wasn't a big fan, but spending the last month of her life in one with her hammered the final nail in the coffin.

When the front doors whooshed open, the vision of him leaving Carol's hospital, broken and alone flooded his mind.

Justin stepped out of the hospital in a daze. Why had no one been here with him? No one came to say goodbye to Carol. Her parents were dead, so that made sense, but he had family. Where were they? Busy had been Liz's reply, and okay, she was planning her own wedding but still... She couldn't take three days off to be here with him? His mother was still in rehab, so she had a decent excuse. She had stopped drinking for years, but when Ryan died last year, she picked it up again. And Peter was filming, so Justin understood that, but Garrett? Yes, he was at med school, but again, he couldn't spare a few days for his only brother? Of course, some of the blame rested on him as well. He hadn't told them how alone he felt. He'd inferred he could handle it all on his own, but he hadn't meant it. He'd assumed they would see through his bravado and come anyway, but they hadn't.

The pastor of their church visited, but Justin didn't know him well, and he hadn't stayed long. Nor had he imparted much wisdom. "She's in a better place." He'd said it as if it made all the sense in the world, but it didn't. Not to Justin who needed her here. Maybe she was in a better place, but he certainly wasn't. Not without her.

He lifted his face to the sky and raised his fist. "I hate you God. Do you hear me? I hate you for taking Carol, and I'll never follow Your words again as long as I live." His voice echoed in the covered area and his own words attacked him like daggers. In despair, he sank down onto the nearby bench and dropped his head into his hands. There he let the tears flow not caring who saw. No one stopped to ask if he was okay. No one placed a hand on his shoulder. No one was there.

Justin forced his mind back to the present and reminded himself this was not Carol's hospital, and he did not have the hurt loved one, but Ava did. He may have had no one there for him, but he was here for Ava, and he could do this!

"Can I help you?" A woman at the information desk called out to them.

"We're here to see my dad. Bruce McDermott? They brought him in after a heart attack." Ava's voice was small and hesitant, so unlike the fearless woman he met just a few weeks ago.

The employee, a smart looking woman with short brown hair and kind eyes, smiled at Ava before turning to the computer beside her and tapping a few buttons. "Yep, there he is. He's still in ICU, but you can at least get to the ICU waiting room and then see when they'll let you back. Let me just get your visitor tags and you can go on up. Can I get your names?"

"Ava and Justin."

"Great, thank you." She tapped a few more buttons, and a moment later, an ancient printer sputtered to life, grunting and groaning as if on its last leg. It spat out two squares which the woman peeled off and handed to them. "Be sure to keep these on while you're in the hospital or you'll find yourselves escorted out."

Ava nodded and pressed her name tag to her chest. Justin followed suit trying not to remember the last time he had done this. He took another calming breath and led Ava to the elevators across the lobby. The silent ride pressed on Justin making him wish he had words to say, but all that kept playing in his head was "she's in a better place." That didn't fit Ava's situation because her father wasn't dead yet. At least he hoped he wasn't, and Justin knew he would never utter those words even if her father died. They hadn't helped him, and he would rather say nothing and just be there for her than issue the empty words he received when Carol died.

The elevator dinged and the doors opened revealing a floor that looked like all the rest - sterile and white with only numbers and arrows to tell you which way to go. He followed her to the right and put his hand on the small of her back when she stopped in front of the frosted glass door labeled Intensive Care Unit.

"I'm right here with you," he whispered hoping he would be able to keep that promise. The room crowded in on him, and he wasn't sure how much longer he would be able to stay, but he sensed she needed strength to open the door and face the waiting game inside.

She nodded, took a deep breath, and pushed the door open.

~

The first thing Ava saw was her mother. Was it her imagination or had she aged ten years in an afternoon? Worry lay on her face like a mask, and her shoulders rolled forward, pushed down by an invisible weight. Ava wondered if she looked the same.

Her mother caught her eye, recognition flaring seconds later, and she bolted out of her seat and across the lobby. "Ava, I'm so glad you're here."

Ava let herself be embraced. Even though she knew her mother hurt as well, a comfort existed just being in her mother's arms. She wrapped her arms around her mother's waist, returning the hug, unsure who needed it more. "How is he, Mom? Have you heard anything?"

Her mother shook her head as she pulled back. Her hands stayed on Ava's upper arms as if she feared Ava might disappear if they weren't touching in some way. "No, we've only been here an hour or so. I haven't spoken with a doctor yet. They took your dad to run some tests."

Her mother's eyes flicked to Justin; the unspoken question evident in her gaze. "I'm so sorry, Justin," Ava said turning to him. For a moment she'd forgotten he stood there, and he clearly looked as if he'd rather be anywhere else. "Mom, this is Justin. Justin, my mom, Selene."

Her mother held out a hand to Justin. "Justin, it's nice to meet you though I'm sorry it had to be here."

"It's a pleasure to meet you as well, Selene."

It hit Ava then the consequences of letting him bring

her. He was now meeting her mother. He might meet her father, and brother and sister if they arrived. Would they quiz her about him? What would she say about his relationship with God or more accurately his lack of a relationship? Her parents had always strongly advised against dating a non-believer, and Ava had taken that advice. Until now. And then there was his anger at her. He'd obviously pushed it aside to help her, but would it come back?

It was never supposed to go this far. He was never supposed to be meeting her family. Her plan had been to keep him away until after their fake relationship ran its course and then explain to her parents that they just didn't have enough in common. All of that flew out the window now.

"Mrs. McDermott?"

Ava turned to the doctor she hadn't even heard approach. He looked young, barely older than herself. Was he capable of working on her father?

"I'm Selene McDermott." Her mother grasped Ava's hand and squeezed.

"Your husband is stable, but there appears to be some blockage to his heart. We'll want to evaluate again tomorrow to see how it looks after the drugs relax the muscle, but he may need bypass surgery. However, we'll discuss that more in detail at a later time. He's still sleeping off the medicine, but you can see him now if you'd like."

"Yes, please. Can we all go?" her mother asked looking first to Ava and then to Justin.

"Immediate family only. He's still weak and he doesn't need any surprises or unsettling events."

Ava turned to Justin. She didn't want to leave him alone, especially since he'd been kind enough to drive her here, but she wanted to see her dad. No, she *needed* to see him, to convince herself that he was alive and okay.

"Go ahead," Justin said as if reading her mind. "I'm not a big fan of hospital rooms anyway. I'll go for a walk and meet you back here."

She opened her mouth to thank him and paused as the words froze in her throat. The meaning behind his words clicked in her brain, and she looked at him - really looked at him. There was a stiffness to his jaw that was unusual even for him and a light sheen of sweat glistened on his forehead. He'd said his first wife had died, but she had never asked for the details. Had she died in a hospital? Was that why he looked so stressed? And yet he'd come with her anyway? Why?

Before she could ponder the questions further, her mother tugged on her arm. "Thank you," she managed to mouth to Justin before she was whisked down the hall.

CHAPTER 18

*J*ustin waited until they disappeared from sight before sinking down into a chair. His head dropped into his hands, and his fingers raked through his hair probably making it a mess, but he didn't care. He'd tried so hard to overcome the fear he had of hospitals and tonight he had succeeded. He had overcome his fear and found the courage to support Ava. But as soon as he sank into the cushions every ounce of courage vanished, drained out and replaced once again by foreboding and dread.

His mind swirled back to eight years ago and the night when he'd held Carol's hand and waited until the beeping stopped.

His back and butt ached from sitting in the hard plastic chair as long as he had, but he didn't dare move. The doctors said it could be any minute, and he would not let Carol die alone. He would not let her take her last breath without him by her side.

A soft crinkle sound grabbed his attention and he lifted his face. Carol's lips twitched - probably the closest thing to a smile she could muster at the moment. Her eyes, clear of the cloudy fog they'd held the last week, caught his.

"Promise me," she wheezed grabbing his hand and holding him tight in her gaze. "Promise me you won't give up on love."

How could he promise that? How could she ask him? She knew that she was the only woman for him. He couldn't even think about loving anyone else, and he opened his mouth to tell her that, but what came out was, "I promise."

He promised though he couldn't imagine loving anyone the way he loved Carol. He promised because she needed to hear it. She needed to know he'd be okay when she was gone, and he did it as his last gift to her.

A tear snaked down his cheek as the pain from so long ago washed over him anew. What would she say if she saw him now? She would be livid. Angry that he'd broken his promise to her but even angrier that he had given up on love.

Carol had been the epitome of an optimist. In fact, she and Ava would probably have been great friends had they known each other.

"Justin, is that you?"

Justin turned surprised to see the woman from the cottage. What had her name been? Mabel? Margaret? Margie? Yes, he thought it was Margie. "Margie, what are you doing here?"

"I volunteer here when I can. I bring flowers to folks and read stories to the children. Mostly I listen. You look like you need a friendly ear and a good listen. Want to lay your troubles at my feet?"

"I have no idea," he said with a sigh. "Suddenly everything I thought made sense in my life no longer makes sense."

Margie sat down next to him. "I think we find that often in life. Are you here with a family member?"

Justin chuckled sadly. "No, I'm here with Ava. Her father had a heart attack."

"Ah, yes," Margie said with a nod. "Heart attacks are hard, but so is being in a hospital when you have strong memories of grief isn't it?"

Justin looked up at the woman. Was she a mind reader? "How could you-"

"I've also been doing this a long time. I've come to recognize the signs. Tell me who you lost."

Justin took a deep breath and blinked to keep the tears building up from spilling over. "My wife died of cancer in a hospital like this one, and I don't think I've ever really gotten over it."

"I don't think one can actually get over the death of a loved one. What they can do is learn to live without them especially if they have the knowledge they will see them again. Were you and your wife believers?"

"She was, and I assumed I was, but I haven't spoken to God since the day she died."

Margie nodded. "That's also understandable. God wants us to talk to Him and take our problems to Him, but He also understands our hurt and anger. And it doesn't matter how long it takes, He is always waiting for us with open arms."

Justin could almost feel the loving arms wrapping around him and lifting the burden. A welcoming voice accompanied them and called him home. He knew what he had to do. "Do they have a chapel in this hospital?"

~

*T*ears pushed against Ava's eyes as she stared at her father. The man who had always been her rock - strong and courageous - now looked so small in the hospital bed. An oxygen tube sat under his nose and other wires ran out of his arms - an IV, a monitor of some sort, who knew what else. With the sheet covering most of him and only these pieces showing, he almost appeared half machine, like something out of a science fiction novel.

His chest rose and fell almost in time with the soft beeping that came from the heart monitor machine in the room, but Ava kept expecting it to stop suddenly at any moment. Her breath caught with every pause and only released again with the next movement of his chest. What would she do if her father died? How would her mother cope? Who would plan the funeral?

Her mother sat next to her father, stroking his hand. Eyes closed, her mouth moved silently and Ava realized she was praying. She should be praying too, but the only phrase in her mind was 'Please don't let him die.' Had Justin felt this way? Suddenly, she understood how he might give up on love. She felt as if a large piece of her were missing already and her father was still breathing. How different would it be if he never woke up?

"Ava, you should probably go check on your boyfriend."

Her mother's voice pulled her back to reality, but it took a moment for the words to register in Ava's mind. "What? Oh, yeah, I suppose, but he's not really my boyfriend Mom."

What was she doing? She wasn't supposed to mention the fake relationship to anyone, least of all her mother, but she just couldn't lie. Not while her father lay in a hospital bed. And she was pretty sure Justin had broken it off anyway.

"What do you mean?" her mother asked.

Ava sighed. "I met Justin a few weeks ago. The story I told on The Evening Show was mostly true. We did both get booked into the same cottage, but while we were there, he found out his image had taken a hit because of his views on love-"

Her mother held up a hand to pause Ava's diatribe. "What do you mean his views on love?"

"Evidently, he's not a big fan, but he hosts a dating show, so he needs it to seem that he is." Her mother shook her head in confusion but motioned Ava to continue. "His boss thought it would improve his image if he was seen in a relationship, but he wasn't in one, so he asked me."

"He asked you to be in a relationship with him?" Her mother's words spilled out slow and haltingly.

"No, he asked me to *pretend* to be in a relationship with him." Ava understood it was a lot to take in, but she thought her mother had been following the thread better than her face showed she was.

"Why would you pretend to be in a relationship with someone? Why not just date for real?"

Ava rolled her eyes. "I do date Mom, but no one's been able to compare to what you and Dad have." She shrugged. "I want that perfect love."

Her mother sucked in her breath and exhaled slowly pinching her lips together. "Is that what you think? That we're perfect?"

"Of course. You guys are still in love, you never fight, you have so much in common." Why was she having to explain this to her mother?

"Because we work at it, Ava. We didn't start out that way. Your dad wasn't even a Christian when I started dating him."

Ava blinked at her mother. "What? But then why would you tell me to only date believers?"

"Because it's what God said to do, and because it's easier. Ava, I was headstrong, and I fell for your father and thought I could change him. Luckily for me, it worked out that way, but it often doesn't. Usually the believer ends up distancing themselves from God. Your father and I didn't want that for you or your brother or sister. That's why we stressed the importance of dating a believer. And you're right, your father and I are still in love, but there were a few years there where we almost split apart."

"What?" It seemed to be the only coherent word Ava could manage and suddenly she needed to sit down. Her entire world had just turned upside down, and her legs didn't feel strong enough to keep holding her up. She backed up to the other chair in the room and sank down.

Her mother walked around the bed to her side. "Ava, your dad and I had the same issues that every couple has. We got married and then wondered if we'd made a mistake. Your father loves to talk to people and I was more of a homebody. I used to get so angry when he would be late for dinner. He would get to talking to someone and forget to call, and I would be sitting at home watching the dinner grow cold alone. It always felt like he was choosing others over me. That frustrated me, and for a few years we fought constantly."

"How did you get through it?"

"We learned how to live together. I learned that I couldn't change your father - he was going to talk to people no matter what I did. So, I would tell him dinner would be ready half an hour before it really was. He made it home on time more often that way, and I also let it go if he was late. I ate dinner alone and packed up leftovers for him. A few nights of cold dinners alone, and he began making an effort to remember to call me if he got caught up. The point is, we figured out how to work together. It wasn't seamless."

Ava shook her head. All this time, she'd thought her parents were perfect. How many good relationships had she walked away from simply because they weren't perfect? "Why did you never tell me?"

Her mother smiled and took her hand. "I thought it was evident, Ava, but now I see we should have been clearer about our relationship. Fairy tale romances are just that - fairy tales. Relationships, and marriage in particular, take work. They are messy and complicated and impossible without God's help. Now, do you want to tell me why you aren't dating Justin for real?"

A soft snort escaped Ava's lips. "I told you Mom, it's a fake relationship. Besides, we are way too different, and I may have pushed him away."

"Oh, I doubt you've pushed him away. At least not for good, and I think something might have changed while you weren't looking. The man drove you all the way out here, and the expression on his face was not the look of a man who hated love but of a man *in* love."

"No, he might have been yesterday, but then I had to go and meddle with things."

"Whatever you meddled with, you can ask for forgiveness. That's also a part of relationships. You will make mistakes. So will he. You just have to learn to ask for forgiveness when you do."

Her mother was right. "I should go find him."

"Yes, I think you should."

CHAPTER 19

*J*ustin stared at the cross in the little chapel. He hadn't needed to go to the chapel to ask God to forgive him, but he'd wanted to. Standing near a cross had once held a special meaning to him, and the power covered him again as he dropped to his knees.

"Lord, I'm so sorry. I've been angry at you for so long that I am unsure how to talk to you anymore. I've shut you out and tried to live life my way, but it's not working. The anger is eating me up inside. Help me not to be so angry. Help me open the doors and let you back in." He was sure there was more he needed to say, but the words wouldn't form, so he let his heart do the talking for him.

When he had poured out everything he had, he opened his eyes and stood. "Thank you," he said to the chaplain who stood off to the side.

"You are most welcome. Is there anything else I can do for you?"

Justin ran a hand across his chin. "Yeah, can you tell me where I might get my bone marrow tested?"

The chaplain tilted his head as he thought. "I think our oncologist could help you. Let me get you his name." He disappeared through a doorway and returned a moment later with a white business card.

Justin took the card and tucked it in his pocket. He would get tested but before he did that, he needed to check on Ava and apologize to her. She was probably still with her father, but if not, she would wonder where he was.

The waiting room was still empty when he opened the door, but a moment later, Ava appeared down the hallway. She smiled when she saw him, but it wasn't her normal smile. It was tentative, hesitant, and much tighter than normal. Did that mean bad news then?

"Hey, I'm glad you're still here," she said when she reached him.

He grabbed her hands and squeezed. "Of course I am. I wouldn't leave without telling you. How's your father?"

She shrugged and wiped the corner of her eye. Justin saw the wet sheen on her finger before she rubbed it away. "He's still out, and he doesn't look like my dad at all, but I'm trying not to worry."

He moved his hands to interlock his fingers with hers. "That's good. I'm sure he will be okay. Heart attacks are scary but they happen a lot, and trained doctors understand how to treat them."

"They are…." she said slowly and Justin felt the 'but' coming before it left her lips, "but it made me realize how short life is. I know we said this wasn't forever, but I want to get married and have a family of my own."

Justin opened his mouth to agree with her, but she continued, "I had a great discussion with my mother, and I understand now that love isn't perfect, and I've been pushing people away for the wrong reasons, but it also made me realize the right reason."

Though she paused, he didn't say what was on his mind because it was clear she needed to get this out. Instead, he took her bait and asked, "What's the right reason?"

"They need to have a relationship with God. My mom told me their marriage was actually rocky for a while and it was only their faith in God that got them through it, so that's my line, and I won't cross it. I'm sorry for going to your brother, and I hope we've done enough to save your image, Justin, but I can't pretend to be your girlfriend any longer."

Justin bit back his smile. She thought she had the upper hand, but she didn't know he'd had his own epiphany as well. "I forgive you for going to Garrett, and I hope you'll forgive me for my anger earlier. It was misplaced. I was putting my anger at Candy on you, and that wasn't fair. Now, about this relationship issue... How about we stop pretending and you be my girlfriend for real?"

She blinked at him. "Did you not hear what I just said? I care for you Justin, more than I should, and I forgive you, but I want someone who will pray with me, attend church with me, and have devotionals with me. You told me you haven't spoken to God in years."

"And I hadn't, but I just came from the chapel. Ava, being here reminded me of Carol dying. The last thing she did was make me promise not to give up on love, but I had. Being here forced me to realize how unhappy I've been, and while I was waiting for you, Margie approached me. Evidently she volunteers here. She helped me see that part of that unhappiness was giving up on love, but the other part was giving up on God. So, I asked Him to forgive me and help me get over my anger and I'm going to get my bone marrow tested to see if I can help Garrett."

Her eyes widened. "You are?"

He nodded. "It's the right thing to do, and you were right. I'd never forgive myself if I could've helped Garrett and didn't. I'm still hurt and angry at them both, but I'm willing to work on letting it go, and I'm hoping you'll help me with that."

"Me?"

"Yes you. You've turned my world upside down since I met you, and now I can't imagine you not in it. You even got me to relax about my hair."

She smiled as she ran a hand through it. "We've still got some work to do there."

"What do you mean? I know it's crazy looking right now and probably because I only used half a can today instead of the whole can."

She giggled and moved her hand to his neck. "That's a start. And can we talk about the jeans?"

He glanced down at his pants. "What about my jeans?"

"They have a permanent crease, Justin. Who irons blue jeans?" Her other hand joined the first around his neck and he moved his arms to the small of her back.

"You mean that's not a thing?" He lowered his head slightly bridging the gap between their lips.

"That is most definitely not a thing." Her eyes held his as her lips parted in invitation.

"Then I guess it's a good thing I have you to help me." He pressed his lips against hers savoring the softness of the kiss. The first kiss had surprised him, the second one had sent his body tingling, but this kiss was the best yet. He let the emotions run through his body waking up areas that had lain dormant for years - his toes, the tips of his ears - every nerve ending tingled, and he allowed the light to sweep away the darkness he'd been living in for too long.

～

"*A*va, he's awake!"

Her mother's voice ripped them apart and dissolved the electricity coursing through Ava's veins. As if guilty, they jumped apart, but her mother either didn't care or didn't notice.

Ava's heart still pounded in her head as she followed her mother back to her father's room, and she forced herself to breathe slowly. She could feel Justin behind her, this masculine presence that sent her knees shaking, but she couldn't focus on that now. Her dad was awake, and she needed to focus on him.

"Sorry if I scared you." Her father pulled the oxygen out of his nose as she reached his bedside. His voice was so quiet and so unlike his normal deep timbre that Ava wasn't sure he had actually spoken until his eyes found hers.

"Dad," she placed her hand on his arm, "are you okay?"

"I guess that depends on how you define okay," he said slowly. "My chest feels like someone dropped an anvil on it." The corner of his mouth twitched into a small smile. "Better than feeling nothing though I guess."

"Dad, don't kid about stuff like that," Ava said. "It's not funny."

"Relax honey, I'll be fine."

"I don't know about that, Bruce," her mother spoke up. "The doctors are talking about bypass surgery. I told you to stop smoking those cigars."

"I'm sure the cigars aren't all to blame," her father said.

"No, but they certainly don't help. You have to eat better, Dad."

"Okay, I will." His eyes flicked to Justin behind her. "Are you going to introduce me to your friend?"

"Oh, um, right. Dad, this is Justin. He's my.... Boyfriend?"

"Is that supposed to be a question?" He looked to Ava and then to Selene.

"It's complicated, sir," Justin said, "but let's just say that we are sure now."

"I'll fill you in on it later," Selene said placing a hand on his arm. "For now, I think we should let you rest."

"We should probably be heading back anyway. I have a test to do, and you have a book to finish."

Ava nodded, but she didn't feel ready to leave. Even though her father was awake and talking, it didn't diminish her fear that something might happen to him afterwards. "You go ahead. I'm going to stay with my dad."

"No, you aren't," her father said. "I'm fine, and you have a book to finish. Let the man take you home. You can always come back later if you feel the need."

Ava took a deep breath. She didn't want to leave her father, but she wasn't going to argue with him especially not while he was in a hospital bed. The last thing she wanted to do was bring any more stress to his heart. In addition, she was behind on her book and needed to finish it, and Justin had been kind enough to drive her here. She couldn't keep him hostage here forever.

After leaning in to give her father one more hug, she followed Justin back to his car praying that everything would be okay with her father.

CHAPTER 20

*J*ustin grimaced as he shrugged back into his shirt. The bone marrow aspiration had been painful and even after the numbing, he'd still felt a stinging sensation.

"Keep the site clean, but don't get it wet for twenty-four hours," the nurse said as she handed him his discharge papers.

"Okay, and you will let me know if I'm a match for Garrett?"

The nurse offered a small smile. "Of course. As soon as we know we'll call you back in. You are doing an amazing thing."

"Thanks." Justin grabbed his things, thanked the nurse, and headed for the exit sign. He tapped in Ava's number to see if she wanted to grab dinner, but before he hit send, a voice grabbed his attention.

"Justin?"

Justin lifted his eyes from his phone to find his brother staring at him. He'd hoped to avoid running into Garrett, but he'd known it might be a possibility. "Hey Garrett."

"What are you doing here?"

Justin shrugged trying not to focus on how sick Garrett looked. His clothes hung on him and his skin was an ashy color. "Liz told me you needed more bone marrow."

"And she told me you said no."

"I had and then an encounter with God and a lovely woman changed my mind. In fact, I believe you've met her. I'm still working on forgiving you, but I would never forgive myself if I could have helped and didn't."

Garrett's eyes glistened, and he ran a hand across his chin. "Thank you, and in case Ava didn't tell you, you were right about Candy. She left me a year ago when I first got sick. Said she couldn't handle playing nursemaid."

"Why didn't you say anything?"

"I tried to, but you wouldn't listen. I should never have chosen a woman over my own brother. I'm so sorry, man."

Justin saw that Garrett was barely holding it together and compassion welled up inside him. Suddenly he saw his brother as he believed God saw him. He'd made a mistake, but Justin had too. Justin had turned his back on his creator for years, and yet God forgave him. Surely, he could do the same for his brother who not only was hurting but had been hurt by the same woman.

He placed a hand on Garrett's shoulder. "I'm sorry too. I shouldn't have shut you out of my life. We all make mistakes, and mine was punishing you. I can't get that year back, but we can kick this thing together and have years to come in the future."

Hope glistened in Garrett's eyes and Justin pulled him in for a hug. He only hoped they would have time to reconnect.

~

*A*va glanced around at the small gathering of friends and smiled. She'd organized this little get together to celebrate her father being released from the hospital following his bypass surgery and Justin's recovery from the bone marrow transplant, but it also served nicely as a way to introduce him to her family and meet his friends. "I'm going to get a drink. Would anyone else like one?"

"I'll help you," Justin said putting his hands against the chair arms.

Ava pushed gently on Justin's shoulders to keep him from getting up. "Nope, not you. You are supposed to be taking it easy. I will bring your drink to you."

"I'm fine, Ava," he grumbled. "It's been four days."

"And the directions say you should rest for five to seven days. I'm just trying to follow the rules and the schedule you've been given." He was so stubborn sometimes, but she could be just as stubborn. She leaned over and kissed him on the cheek.

Peter laughed and lifted his drink in salute. "She's got you there, Justin."

Justin crossed his arms and leaned back in the chair. "It's a recommendation, not a schedule."

His scowl did nothing but enlarge her smile as Ava knew he enjoyed being taken care of. Justin, like most men, morphed into the biggest baby when he wasn't feeling well. She'd spent the last four days at his house working so she could help him out until he was one hundred percent cleared. Peter had offered to take the nights, and while Ava was tiring of playing nursemaid, she had enjoyed the time with Justin.

It allowed their relationship to progress, and he'd even helped her finish her book. It was nice to have a man's opinion on it, and it turned out they had more than just a love of the ocean and Code Red Mountain Dew in common. They also both loved to play scrabble (she usually clobbered him) and solitaire (he always smoked her time). They both enjoyed walks though those were on hiatus until Justin was cleared, and they both preferred cats over dogs.

Ava would never have thought it possible, but Justin had changed so much since letting God back in his life that she could even see a long-term future with him. Sure, he still used a little too much hairspray, and he'd cringed the first time she handed him jeans with no creases, but those were small things.

"There you are," she said to Gen as she entered the kitchen. "I've been looking for you."

Gen looked up from the drink she was sipping. "I came in to check my email and do I have news for you."

Ava crossed to the fridge and pulled out the punch to refill hers and Justin's cups. "What news?"

"The publishing company loves your new book."

"That's great."

"And they want to offer an advance on your next book." Gen squealed and turned the phone so Ava could see the screen as well.

"What?" Ava's eyes scanned the email. "I can't believe it."

"I can. I told you that you were an amazing author. You just needed to believe it yourself."

~

*J*ustin smiled as Ava approached, but he could tell something was on her mind. Tiny creases dotted her forehead that weren't normally there and an expression he couldn't place lay across her face.

"Everything okay?" he asked as he took his cup.

"Yeah, I just found out that my publishers are offering an advance for my next book."

Before she could stop him, Justin pushed himself up and wrapped his arms around her. "That's amazing. I knew you were an amazing author, and you deserve it."

"I just didn't expect it. I never thought I'd be given that kind of money as an advance."

"Ahem," Peter cleared his throat and the attention in the room shifted to him. "If we're sharing news, I have some of my own. I've been approached by MDR Studios to produce a new romantic sitcom, and I've said yes."

Justin's jaw fell open. He had always thought he would be the one to leave the show first, but now Peter would be. "What does that mean for Who Wants to Marry a Cowboy?" Of course, what he really meant was, what does that mean for me?

"I was going to talk to you about that. There are two options for you. One, you can continue the show either as the producer or host or both-" Justin wasn't sure he liked that option. Peter was the only reason he had stayed on the show as long as he had. "Or two, you can come be my lead actor."

"You have the power to offer me that role without even an audition?" Justin's head was spinning. Acting had always been his dream, but hosting had been as close as he'd gotten.

"It was part of my conditions. I told them I wanted to have the decision on the lead actor and the lead writer. I was hoping maybe Ava would like to take a chance writing for the sitcom as well."

"What?" Ava's mouth had fallen open and her wide eyes stared at Peter without blinking.

"I read your book - the newest one as well as your first. You're funny, and you would make a great scene writer. I'd be honored if you'd write for me, and you'd still have time to write your books on the side."

"I don't know what to say."

"Say yes," Justin said with a smile, "because I'm going to."

She looked from Justin to Peter to Gen. "Okay, yes."

"This calls for a toast. Who's got champagne?" Ava's father shouted over the cheers and congratulations.

"Not for you Dad. You're still recovering and I don't think champagne is on your new diet."

"You're such a stickler," he said and Justin smiled as he looked around the room. How different his life had become in just a few short weeks. He was mending the relationship with his brother, he had a new job offer he was excited about, and he had the love of an amazing woman whom he never would have met if it hadn't been for Peter and a scatter-brained woman named Margie.

Margie. Of course. The plan began to formulate in his head.

*a*va smiled as she recognized the familiar landscape. Justin claimed he was taking her somewhere special and she had expected a nice restaurant, but she hadn't expected him to drive them back to the cottage where they met. For someone who claimed he hated romance, he certainly was good at the little gestures.

"Going back to the scene of the crime, are you?"

He glanced at her. "Something like that."

"I guess you got the keys already," she said as he bypassed the rental office and continued down the twisty road that led to the ocean. Had he called ahead then?

He said nothing but flashed her a quick smile. Okay, he would make her wait. She could do that.

A few minutes later, he pulled the car to a stop in front of the 'slice of tranquility' cottage. Before she made a move to open her door, he turned off the car and bounded out to open the door for her. Ever since he'd been cleared after the transplant, he appeared to be more active than even before.

She took his hand and followed him inside. The lights in the cottage were off but the soft glow of candlelight illuminated the room and rose petals littered the floor. What was all this?

He led the way to the kitchen where candles, flowers, and two bottles of Code Red Mountain Dew covered the table. Ava grinned up at him. "Mountain Dew, really?"

"Well, it's what brought us together originally."

"I knew you were a romantic at heart," she said wrapping her arm around his waist.

"I had a very good teacher," he returned kissing her forehead. "There's a box there for you."

"A box?" Ava cocked her eyebrow at him but stepped up to the table. Nestled in the middle of a bouquet of flowers lay a small black box. Was he proposing? She plucked the box out and turned to him with wide eyes.

"Open it," he said with a smile.

Ava popped the lid open and gasped. Inside was a diamond ring. It appeared to be at least a carat by the size of it and it sent rainbows of colors cascading in every direction.

"I know we haven't known each other that long, but I can't imagine you not in my life Ava McDermott."

"Justin, I..." she trailed off as her words died in her throat.

"You asked me once what those two couples on the show had that made them last."

Ava nodded. She remembered the question from the day they'd met.

"It was their faith in God. I do believe all the couples on our show have been in love, but when they leave, they have nothing solid to build a life upon. Tyler and Laney and the couple before them both had a foundation in God. That's why they lasted and why we will too."

"You really believe that?" Ava had thought of her perfect proposal often and though this wasn't exactly what she had imagined - waves lapping the sunset kissed beach, the man on his knee confessing his undying love - this was even better. Perfect because it was so personal to them.

"I really do. I want to spend the rest of my life with the woman who makes me laugh, who challenges me, who spurs me to be a better man and the woman I love with my whole heart."

Ava wanted all that too. And she'd known for some time that she wouldn't want it with anyone but Justin. She was ready to marry him and start a family. She pulled the ring from the box, but before she could place it on her finger, he took it and slid it down her ring finger. "I love you too, and I can't wait to marry you."

As Justin leaned in to kiss her, Ava heard the sound of a camera flash. She pulled back, surprised to see Margie standing a few feet away with an old Polaroid camera. "Margie?"

"Yep, that one is going to look perfect on my wall," the woman said as she waved the small square back and forth.

"What's going on?" Ava asked looking from Justin to Margie.

Justin grinned. "It turns out our getting double booked here wasn't really a coincidence after all."

"What?" Ava felt like the world had shifted all of a sudden into an alternate reality.

Margie shrugged. "I'm kind of a matchmaker."

"I don't understand."

"I pray about all the people who book with me, and if God tells me to, I double book them. He told me about you two. I have to say I wasn't sure when I saw the two of you, but like always, He was right."

Ava laughed and shook her head. If anyone else had told her this story, she wouldn't have believed it, but somehow with Margie, she could. "So, I guess this means you have to come to the wedding now."

Margie laughed and Justin pulled Ava in for the kiss that had been interrupted. Ava heard the camera click again, but she didn't mind. There was no place she would rather be.

EPILOGUE

*A*va smiled as the soft salty breeze lifted her hair. She and Justin both agreed they wanted a beach wedding and what better beach than the one they met on?

The slice of tranquility cottage had served as their dressing rooms allowing her, Kelsie, and Genevieve to get ready. Justin, Garrett, and Peter had gotten ready across the hall, and Margie played referee making sure Justin didn't see Ava until it was time. Ava still wasn't sure if the woman was an angel or just displayed an angelic personality, but she decided it didn't matter.

Now, it was time, and Ava could hardly believe the transformation of the beach. Tiki lights gave the area a soft glow in the setting sun and a hundred white chairs filled the beach. Instead of a red carpet, red rose petals marked the aisle leading up to where Justin stood with the pastor.

"You look beautiful honey," her father said as he leaned in to give her a quick kiss on the cheek. Fully recovered from his bypass surgery, he appeared stronger than ever. Ava was so glad this day had come while he was still around to walk her down the aisle.

The music started and Genevieve and Peter began their walk down the aisle. Kelsie and Garrett went next, and Ava marveled at how healthy Garrett looked. At least twenty extra pounds sat on his frame and his color had returned to a healthy glow instead of the sickly pallor that laid on his face the first day she met him.

"Are you ready?" her father asked as the music shifted.

"I feel like I've been ready for most of my life," Ava said with a smile. She put her free hand on her father's arm and began the march down the aisle.

"Who gives this woman away?" the pastor asked when they reached the front.

"Her mother and I do." Her father patted her hand before placing it in Justin's outstretched palm.

At Justin's touch, a tingle shot up Ava's arm. She would never have believed that first day that they would be getting married, but God worked in mysterious ways and with unusual people sometimes.

"Do you Ava McDermott take Justin Miller to be your husband till death do you part?" the pastor asked.

"I do."

"Do you Justin Miller take Ava McDermott to be your wife till death do you part?"

"I do," Justin said with a smile.

"Then by the power vested to me by the great state of

California, I now pronounce you husband and wife. You may kiss your bride."

The crowd behind them cheered as Justin leaned in and kissed Ava. Her first kiss as a married woman. It was as good as she had expected it would be, and though she knew it might not always bring fireworks, she rested easy in the knowledge that their faith in God would bring them through any trial they might face.

The End!

PART I
AVA'S BLESSING IN DISGUISE

CHAPTER 1

*A*va rubbed the right side of her neck as she glanced over at her daughter spread eagle in the bed next to her. At four years of age, Kylie normally slept the entire night in her own bed, but for some reason, every night this week she had woken up screaming between three thirty and four thirty. Ava had dutifully walked down the hall and brought the girl back to her bed. Kylie wasn't the easiest person to sleep with as she tended to kick and punch, but Ava got more sleep that way than if she tried to stretch out in the recliner in Kylie's room.

"I sure wish I knew why she keeps waking up," Justin said rubbing his eyes. His voice was heavy with sleep. "I could use some decent sleep."

"Me too. I pray every night for her to sleep through the night." Ava brushed blond curls from Kylie's forehead. "It must be a phase though."

As she rolled over, her hand stole back to her neck

and rubbed the aching part again. She must have slept on it funny. Oh well, she'd call her massage therapist later. He was always telling her to come in more often anyway.

~

"Whoa, what happened to you?" Heidi, her friend and nanny, asked as Ava dropped Kylie off that morning. She'd met Heidi at the day care center she and Justin had chosen three years ago when Ava had decided to go back to writing full time. She loved spending time with Kylie at home, but she'd quickly realized she got no writing done when she had the baby all day, so they had agreed to put Kylie in a center for a few hours so Ava could get work done.

The center had been wonderful, but Heidi had been her favorite employee and when she decided to leave to start her own home center, Ava had willingly followed. Now, she was more like Kylie's aunt and a member of Ava's family than a nanny.

Ava's face scrunched in discomfort and her hand massaged her neck again. "I think I slept on it wrong. When Kylie woke me up this morning – early again," she shot her daughter a pointed look, "I noticed it when I tried to go back to sleep."

Heidi nodded as she pulled a tray of blueberry muffins from the oven. "She took a long nap yesterday."

"Yeah, I don't know why she's been waking up in the

middle of the night, but it's making for a long week." Ava yawned and covered her mouth.

"Well, I hope you get some work done today. Kylie give mommy a hug before she has to go."

"Bye Mommy," Kylie said as she wrapped her little arms around Ava's neck.

"Bye Baby. Be good for Heidi." Ava placed a kiss on her daughter's cheek before heading back to her car. As she climbed inside, a sharp pain shot down her neck. She punched in James's number and put the phone on speaker as she backed out of Heidi's driveway.

"Hey Ava, what can I do for you?" James had been her massage therapist for the last few years. Ava had never realized how much stress she carried in her shoulders until her pregnancy with Kylie. When she'd began suffering from headaches, her doctors had finally told her it was due to the stress in her shoulders. They had referred her to a massage therapist, and she had seen James once a month since then.

"James, I know it's a little early for my regular appointment, but I seemed to have tweaked my neck in my sleep. Is there any chance you have an opening today?"

"I don't think I have anything until after five, but let me check." Ava heard the clacking of computer keys before James came back on the line. "Sorry, Ava. Five pm is my first opening today."

"Okay thanks for checking." Five wouldn't work. Justin was filming today, so she'd have Kylie after three and Kylie would not sit through an hour-long massage. The girl was well-behaved but not that well-behaved. Surely, if she had Gen massage it a little bit, the pain would go away. She'd better stop and get Gen a coffee then. Butter her up a bit.

"To what do I owe this?" Gen asked as Ava placed the tall Caramel Macchiato on her desk.

Ava flashed her most charming, hopeful smile. "I was hoping you would massage my neck a little. I woke up with this slight stiffness and James can't get me in today."

Gen smiled and picked up the cup. "I would have done it for free, but thanks for the coffee." She took a sip before motioning Ava to sit at her desk. "What did you do?" she asked as her hands pressed on Ava's neck.

"I don't know. Slept on it wrong maybe. Kylie was up early again this morning and I noticed it when I tried to go back to sleep." Ava winced as Gen's fingers found the tender spot.

"You should go see Chris. I bet he could adjust you and get this taken care of." Chris was Gen's boyfriend who just happened to be a chiropractor.

"That's a good idea."

"Let me get you his number. I don't mind continuing to work on you, but I'd feel better if a professional looked at you." Gen grabbed a sticky note off Ava's deskpad and scribbled a number on it. "Call Chris."

"Okay, I will." Ava stuck the note on the side of her monitor. She didn't mind chiropractors — she'd been once or twice before — but she wasn't convinced that what they did helped. Maybe if she just tried writing, the pain would disappear and she could avoid going.

She pulled up her current work in progress and read over what she had typed the day before. It was so tempting to work at home, but she'd promised herself when Kylie came along that she would be present when she was home, so she kept her writing mainly for at the office and the occasional evening when she was awake after Kylie went to bed. That wasn't too many nights.

A rambunctious four-year-old not only kept Ava on her toes but wore her out, so that by the time Kylie was lying down, Ava was too exhausted to open her computer. The effect had been that her books took a little longer to release, but it had also forced her to plan them out better so that she didn't waste any writing time.

After she finished reading her words from yesterday, she glanced over her plot line. Ah, yes, that's where she was planning to go next. Her fingers stroked the keys and then the rhythmic tapping began. She grew so focused on the story that the pain in her neck lessened to a dull ache at least until she hit her first wall.

When she removed her fingers and leaned back, the pain reared its ugly head. It was worse than before, and now in addition to the pain, her neck felt stiff. Ava turned it to the right surprised to feel a sharp pain. She tried the left but got the same result. Okay, she might have to give Chris a call after all.

*A*va pulled into the small parking lot of Chris's chiropractic office and parked the car. He had agreed to squeeze her in just before lunch, and she'd taken the appointment. A pain in the neck was one thing, but a stiff neck made her job so much harder.

"Welcome to Caring Chiropractic," the woman behind the desk said as Ava entered. "I'm Virginia."

"Ava Miller. I called ahead to see Chris er Dr. Gibson."

Virginia smiled. "Ah, yes. I have you on the books. Since it's your first time seeing us, I will need you to fill out some paperwork though."

"Of course." Ava had expected nothing less. Everyone wanted forms filled out nowadays, but she supposed she couldn't blame them. With all the lawsuits in the world, it was especially important to have bases covered if you were in the medical profession.

She took the clipboard and the forms to one of the

chairs in the small waiting room and began answering the questions. No, she wasn't injured on the job. At least she didn't think she had been. Yes, the pain was severe. No, it wasn't traveling down her arms or legs. Yes, it was hindering movement. No, she'd had no recent surgeries. In fact, the last time she had been in the hospital was Kylie's birth. No, she had not been in an accident. She circled the area on the diagram that corresponded with her pain and flipped the form over. After reading the legalese, she signed her name consenting to treatment and then returned the clipboard to the desk.

"Ava, if you want to follow me, I'll do a quick consultation before Dr. Gibson sees you."

Ava followed the petite blond woman down the hall to a small room. It held only the adjusting table, a stool, and one chair. Virginia sat down in the stool and motioned for Ava to take the chair. "You drove yourself, right?"

"Yes, though I'm not sure I should have. I had motion this morning, but now my neck is so stiff I can barely turn it." Ava attempted to demonstrate but the pain kept her from turning very much.

"That's fine. I just see that your insurance company requires in house x-rays and Dr. Gibson will want some before he treats you. Do you think you could drive to their clinic and then back here?"

The thought sounded as appealing as getting a root canal, but if it would stop the pain, Ava would do it. "I don't think it's very safe for me to be driving far, but as it's right down the road, I could probably do it."

"Is there someone who could drive you?"

"Yeah, maybe Genevieve. I'll call her and see if she can meet me here."

"Great. I'll put in the order and we'll get you taken care of."

Ava followed Virginia back to the front and while she placed the order, Ava shot off a text to Gen. A few minutes later, Gen entered the office, a harried frown on her face.

"Why didn't you tell me it had gotten worse?" Gen asked as she helped Ava into her Range Rover.

"It came on kinda suddenly. I was working on the book and when I stopped typing, I realized my neck had stiffened." Ava let out a groan as Gen hit a bump in the road.

"Sorry, I'll slow it down and watch for bumps."

Ava closed her eyes and sent a prayer up as Gen continued to drive. 'Lord, please take this pain away. Let it be nothing major and give the doctors the wisdom to fix it.'

"We're here," Gen said a moment later and Ava eased herself out of the car.

Radiology was on the first floor of the clinic and it took only a few minutes to get checked in, but by the time they sat down, Ava's head felt as if it weighed an extra fifty pounds. She leaned over, letting it rest lightly on her hands. It wasn't extremely comfortable, but it eased a little of the burden from her neck.

"Ava Miller?"

"Here." Ava said the word without looking up. That would follow but slowly. "Guess I'll be right back," she said to Gen before following the woman into the bowels of radiology.

"Okay, it looks like we're taking three cervical x-rays today, so I need you to remove your shirt, bra, and any jewelry on your neck or ears." The woman pointed to a folded piece of fabric on a stool. "There's a gown here. Go ahead and put it on but don't worry about tying it. I'll help you with that."

Ava chuckled. She couldn't have tied anything behind her back at the moment if she tried. In fact, she wasn't entirely sure she'd be able to get her shirt and necklace off, but she'd deal with that if it happened.

The woman pulled the curtain closed behind her and Ava took a deep breath before peeling her shirt off. The necklace was a little easier as she was able to turn the clasp to the front of her neck and not have to reach so far, but she wasn't sure she would bother putting it back on. However, she held the golden cross for a moment and whispered another prayer for healing and knowledge before laying it on her shirt. Then she slid her bra off, added it to the pile, and put on the gown.

"Ready?" the technician asked as Ava pulled open the curtain.

"I think so." Ava turned so the woman could tie the back and then she followed the woman into the darkened room just ahead.

"Okay, can you put your left shoulder against this and then hold still?"

"That shouldn't be a problem since I can barely move," Ava said with a small smile.

"I'm so sorry. Hopefully we can figure out what's going on and get you fixed up." The woman moved another piece of the x-ray machine closer to Ava's right side and then disappeared into a small room. Ava heard a hum followed by a beep and then the woman reappeared. "Okay, now if you can put your back against this."

Ava did as she was told but she couldn't get the back of her head completely against the piece the technician pointed to. "Here let me help." The woman pushed gently on Ava's forehead until it rested against the back part. Ava grimaced only slightly and tried not to let the fear overtake her. What was wrong with her?

"Hold there." The woman disappeared again. Another hum, beep, and the woman appeared again. "Okay, last one. It's going to sound weird, but I need you to open your mouth."

Ava had no idea what that position helped them see, but she complied and then the experience was over.

"You need to take these back, correct?"

"Yes ma'am."

"Great. Go ahead and get dressed and head back to the lobby. I'll get them copied to a disk and should have it ready in about five minutes."

"Thank you." Ava stepped back into the small room that held her clothing and redressed placing her necklace in her pocket. Then she headed back to the lobby. As soon as she reached the chair next to Gen, she once again let her head rest on her hands. It felt so heavy and stiff.

Gen placed a hand on her shoulder but said nothing. Ava didn't mind. The gesture alone brought a comfort that words couldn't have anyway.

"Here you are," the technician said a few minutes later and handed Ava an envelope.

Ava tucked it in her purse and thanked the technician before following Gen back to her car.

"Will you be okay if I drop you off?" Gen asked as she fastened her seatbelt. "I need to run some errands."

"Yeah, I'll be fine. I'll probably go home after this and it isn't far." Ava had no idea how the adjustment would go, but it had to be better than what she was feeling now. She rested her head against the headrest in the car and prayed they wouldn't hit any bumps.

When they arrived back at the chiropractor's, Gen helped Ava out of the car. "Be sure to let me know how it goes," she said as she opened the front door for Ava.

"I will, thank you." Ava waved to her friend and then stepped up to the front desk. She handed the envelope to Virginia and then took a seat again.

"Let me just get these loaded up, Ava, and I'll be right back."

"I'll be here," Ava said but she didn't lift her head. It felt better if she could just let her hands hold the weight up.

Virginia disappeared down the hallway, but a moment later she was back again muttering under her breath. "I can't believe they did that. Angela, can you get Radiology on the line for me?"

Uh oh, this didn't sound good. Ava hoped they didn't want her to drive back because she didn't think she would be able to.

"Hi, this is Virginia over at Caring Chiropractic. I just sent a patient over for x-rays. She brought back the film but it's encrypted. I tried her date of birth but that isn't opening it... No, I can't open any part of it... I don't know what to tell you, it says it's encrypted... Okay, well, thank you."

"What's the problem?" Chris's voice joined the conversation.

"They sent the films but they're encrypted. The guy at Ava's clinic just told me that they don't do that. He refused to help me."

"Let's just do the x-rays in house free of charge. If we don't charge for them, we aren't breaking the insurance company's rules."

Ava wanted to thank him. There was no way she could have driven back to the clinic.

"Ava? Come with me?" Ava stood and followed Virginia down the hallway once again. "I'm so sorry about this."

"I'm just glad you have the option to do them in house. I don't think I could have driven back."

Virginia rolled her eyes. "No, and it's ridiculous that that's what they wanted you to do. We'll just get these taken quickly and get you some relief."

"Thank you." Ava followed Virginia's directions and stood still while the x-rays were taken again.

"All right, Ava, all done. Dr. Gibson should be in soon."

Ava sank down in the chair and rested her head once again. She hoped Chris would be able to provide her relief. The pain was getting more intense.

The door opened and Chris entered. "Hey Ava. I'm sorry to see you're in so much pain. You have no idea what you did, huh?"

"No, I just woke up with a slight pain in my neck, but now I can't move it."

"It's probably a pinched nerve, but let me take a look at your x-rays."

Ava used her fingers to tilt her head up slightly so she could see the screen. She had no idea how to read the pictures, but even she could tell that the top vertebrate in her neck didn't look right.

"Yep, right there." Chris pointed at the twisted vertebrate. "Your C1-C4 are very clearly out of alignment. The good news is we can treat you and get you some relief. The bad news is that it's going to take a few days."

The weight that sat on Ava's shoulders grew heavier. "Days?"

"Yeah, I mean I would bet that you'll be about ten percent better tomorrow and another twenty percent the day after. Then when we have you moving again, we can look at why this happened. Okay?"

"Okay." Ten percent wasn't much, but Ava's pain was

so bad now that she would take whatever relief he could give. Even if it was only ten percent.

"Now this is going to hurt today, but it should feel a little better after this adjustment." He held out a hand to help her stand and led her over to the adjustment table. "Let's have you lie down on your back."

"I'm not sure I can," Ava said in a small voice.

"I'll help. Just wrap your arms around my neck."

Ava did as Chris instructed, and he placed a hand behind her neck. The pain hit when she was still a foot from the table and by the time he got her prone, tears filled her eyes.

"I know this hurts and what I'm about to do will hurt even more, but then you should feel better." His hands twisted and pulled at her neck and Ava bit back the scream that wanted to emerge. "Wiggle your left foot," he said and then yanked on her neck.

Pain like she had never felt before flooded her body, and Ava couldn't stop the whimper that escaped her lips. Nor could she stop the tear that trickled out of the corner of her eye.

"I know. One more."

Ava wasn't sure she could take one more, but before she had time to think about it, he had probed and yanked the right side of her neck. The pain burned through her body blacking out her vision for a moment. More tears joined the first cascading down her cheeks.

"I know it hurts, and it's okay to cry. I'll be right back

with an ice pack, and I just want you to lay here for twenty minutes or so."

Ava wasn't sure she could stay in this position another five minutes much less twenty, but she would try. As Chris left the room to get the ice pack, Ava let the tears stream down her face. "Please, Lord, take the pain away."

Chris returned a moment later with the ice pack and slid it under her neck before exiting again, but the pain didn't lessen. Ava felt trapped. She couldn't sit up due to the pain, but she couldn't lay here much longer. Should she scream out? Could they hear her crying? Surely, he would come back in a few minutes. She could last another few minutes.

"How are you doing?" Chris asked a few minutes later as he entered the room again.

"Can I sit up and put the ice on my neck that way?" Ava managed through her tears.

"It's not quite as effective. Is this position bothering you?"

"It hurts so much."

"Okay, let's get you up then."

Ava had no strength to even help push; she was completely reliant on Chris as he put an arm around her and pulled her up. Again, the pain blacked out her vision for a moment.

"There you go. Think you're okay to drive home?"

"Maybe in a minute. The room is still spinning."

"Of course. When you get home, I want you to sit with

this ice pack on. Twenty minutes on and then chill it for forty. Then ice again. Okay?"

Ava agreed but she was beginning to wonder if she would make it home. And if she did, how she would venture out again to get Kylie. She was going to have to call in more favors.

CHAPTER 3

*J*ustin's face was etched with concern when he entered the house that night. "Ava? What's going on?"

She put her fingers to her lips and pointed to Kylie who was curled up on the couch. With a much softer voice she answered his question. "I'm not sure. I woke up a little stiff today and now I can't move my neck."

"Have you been to the doctor?"

"I went and saw Chris. He thinks it's just a pinched nerve."

Justin folded his arms across his chest and raised an eyebrow. "No offense to Chris, but I think you need to see a doctor. What if it's something more serious?"

"I have another adjustment with him tomorrow, but if it's not better, I promise I'll go to the doctor. Now, do you think you can take this little one upstairs to her bed? I'm probably going to sleep here tonight." The painful memory of trying to lay flat at the chiropractor's was still fresh in her mind and Ava had no desire to repeat that. Plus, Justin left earlier in the morning than she did. What if she could lay down but then couldn't get up the next morning? No, it was better to sleep in the recliner and not bother Justin. Besides, the pain was manageable as long as she sat just perfectly in the recliner.

"Yes, I'll get Kylie, and then I'm coming back to check on you."

Ava appreciated his concern, but there was nothing he could do for her. She'd spent the last several hours icing her neck, then sleeping while it chilled again, then icing it again. Afraid to drive more than she had to, she'd asked Gen to pick up Kylie and grab her some food on the way home. Thankfully, Kylie had been willing to spend the evening watching TV on the couch – something Ava rarely let her do most days.

True to his word, Justin returned after scooping Kylie up and dropping her off upstairs. "Is there anything I can do for you?" His eyes roamed over Ava as if unsure where or how to help.

"Can you put this back in the freezer for me?" She handed him the ice pack and grimaced only slightly as her neck readjusted to the slight difference in space with the pack gone.

He took it from her and walked to the kitchen. She heard the freezer door open and close, and then he was in front of her again. "Anything else?"

"Pray with me?" Though Ava had been praying

throughout the day herself, hearing her husband pray over her sounded like exactly the healing she needed.

With a smile, Justin placed his hand on her head. "Lord, we thank you for this day. We thank you for the many blessings you have given us, but tonight we come to you with a request. Please heal Ava's neck – whatever is going on – and give her rest. We know that you are the divine healer and we ask that you would place that healing hand on her. Give her comfort and healing so that she can return to her normal life. In your name we pray, Amen."

"Amen," Ava echoed and she squeezed his hand. "Thank you. I'm sorry I won't be in bed tonight."

Justin leaned down and placed a kiss on her forehead. "You just worry about you and getting the rest you need. Besides if I get too lonely, there's a couch right there I can come claim."

"I love you, Justin Miller."

"And I love you, Ava." He placed another kiss on her cheek and then headed upstairs.

Ava was left in the dark empty living room. Justin often fell asleep down here when he got off work late, but Ava never did, and the eerie quiet pressed in on her. She flicked on the TV and surfed through the channels until she found something she wouldn't mind watching.

At some point her eyes closed, and when she opened them again, the show was over. The clock showed an hour had passed and as Ava's neck was throbbing again, she decided to get the ice pack once more. And maybe some Tylenol. Chris had suggested she go light on the pain killers so that she didn't assume she was better and tweak her neck even more, but at this point Ava doubted two Tylenol would do that for her. She wasn't even sure how much it would dull the pain, but she needed something.

She shuffled into the kitchen and retrieved the ice pack wrapping it in a paper towel to keep it from burning her neck. Then she grabbed the Tylenol from the upper cabinet. Kylie wasn't the type of kid to get into cabinets, but Ava still liked keeping the medicine out of her reach.

Ava flicked the lid off easily but as she stared down at the two white pills in her palm, she wondered how she was going to swallow them. Taking pills was not her specialty and the only way she could generally do it was to fill her mouth with water, tilt her head back, and drop the pills in. But there was no way she could do that in her current condition. She'd have to try something different.

Ava filled her mouth with water and then as carefully as possible, she slid the pills into her mouth. When they were both in, she swallowed, hoping the water would wash them down her throat. She hated the bitter taste of pills in her mouth if they didn't make it down the first time. Thankfully, luck was with her and she felt both pills make it down her throat. After replacing the pill bottle, she grabbed the ice pack and headed back to the recliner.

It took her another few minutes, but finally she was situated just right so that the pain was manageable and she was as comfortable as possible.

∾

"*M*ommy, can I have cereal?"

Ava opened her eyes and turned as much as she could to see her daughter standing next to the recliner. "Yeah Baby. Just give Mommy a second to wake up." A second wouldn't really cut it. Nor would a pot of black coffee. Ava had tossed and turned most of the night either waking up due to the pain or some unknown creak and groan of the house. She would definitely be napping today after getting Kylie dropped off.

Her neck screamed in agony as she righted the recliner and stood. Ava had thought that maybe it was getting a little better yesterday with all the icing, but this morning it seemed even stiffer if that was possible, and a funny pressure in her ears along with a fire when she swallowed had joined the pain in her neck. But she put on a brave face for her daughter.

"Did you sleep good Pumpkin?" She ruffled her daughter's blond curls as she crossed to the kitchen.

"Yeah, I didn't dream though."

"Well, we don't always dream, so that's not always a bad thing. Did you want cereal this morning?"

"Uh huh, the cinnamon kind."

Ava retrieved a bowl and then grabbed the cereal from the pantry. With her daughter taken care of, she turned her attention to the coffee pot. She had never drunk coffee until she met Justin, but his pot a day habit had started to slowly rub off on her, and now she found she craved a cup or two in the morning. Thankfully, her stomach seemed to hit its coffee limit at two cups which was usually fine with Ava. Today though she wished it would tolerate more because she wasn't sure how she would function on just two cups.

"Are you going to take a shower today, Mommy?" Kylie asked before shoveling in a large spoonful of cereal.

Ava grimaced at the thought. It had been hard enough washing her hair yesterday morning and she'd had limited movement then. She had none today and couldn't imagine how challenging it would prove this morning. "I think I'll skip it today. Mommy has to take off work today and rest anyway."

Kylie's face lit up. "Can I stay home with you Mommy?"

"Oh, baby, I'd love that, but Mommy has to go see the doctor again to see if he can fix my neck. Then I'll probably sleep most of the day. I wouldn't be much fun today."

Kylie's lips pushed out in a pout. "Okay, Mommy, but we'll have a playday soon, right?"

"Of course we will." Ava hoped she wasn't lying to her daughter. The thought of anything more than sitting in her chair all day sent her stomach curling in on itself, but surely another adjustment today would have her neck feeling better.

After a quick breakfast for herself and a change of clothes for both of them, Ava herded Kylie out to the car. "Can you climb up today, baby? Because Mommy cannot lift you."

"Sure I can, Mommy. I'm four now, remember?" Said in her matter of fact voice, Ava couldn't help but smile as she watched her daughter climb into the car. When had she gotten so big?

Ava eased herself into her own seat trying not to move her neck any more than she had to. The ride to Heidi's was slow and painful, but Ava once again thanked God when she arrived safely. Driving with limited movement was scary, but having her daughter in the car upped her anxiety. She would never forgive herself if she got in an accident with Kylie in the car.

"Whoa, you don't look much better," Heidi said as Ava signed Kylie in.

"No, I'm afraid it isn't much better. I couldn't even lay down last night – had to sleep in the recliner, but I have another adjustment today, so I'm hoping that helps."

"I'll be praying for you." Those five simple words were one of the main reasons Ava and Justin had followed Heidi when she started her in home center. At the other daycare, most of the workers had been believers but because it was a business, they could rarely express their faith, but Heidi worked for herself now and that meant she could be open and vocal about her beliefs. Ava was comforted by the knowledge that Heidi would not only talk to Kylie about God but taught her prayers as well.

"Thank you." Ava glanced down at Kylie wrapped tightly around her leg. "Kylie, honey, it's time to stay with Heidi. She'll take good care of you until Mommy comes back."

"No, I don't want you to leave," Kylie said shaking her head back and forth.

"Kylie, you have to. Mommy has to get her neck fixed again, but I promise I'll be back to get you this afternoon."

"You promise?" Her daughter's wide blue eyes tugged on Ava's heart. She'd thought she was doing a good job hiding her pain, but clearly Kylie could sense something was off. Ava would have to up her game and work on her poker face to assure her daughter.

"I promise baby."

CHAPTER 4

read filled Ava as she pulled into the parking lot of Caring Chiropractic. It wasn't that she disliked seeing Chris or even his employees, but the thought of the adjustment and the pain it would bring again was almost unbearable. She took a deep breath and prayed for courage as she opened the front door of the office.

"Ava, you look better today," Chris said.

"Really? I don't feel any better. I still can't move my neck and I had to sleep in a chair last night."

He nodded as if he'd expected that answer. "Not surprising, but after today's adjustment, you should feel thirty percent better."

Ava scribbled her name on the sign in log. "Is it going to hurt as much as it did yesterday?"

"Probably, but then it will get better. Come on, I'll take

you back before you have too long to think about it." He motioned for her to follow him down the hallway.

"Do we have to do it lying down again?" The fear in Ava's voice surprised her. She didn't normally consider herself a fearful person, but that pain yesterday had been… she didn't even have words for what it had been.

"We can try sitting if you'd like." Chris pulled the chair into the center of the room and patted the back. "Just make sure you put your back all the way against the back of the chair here."

Ava complied and tried to relax as his hands felt around her neck again, but it was impossible. Even with his help in moving her neck, the pain started before he yanked and then skyrocketed off the charts with the swift movement. Not quite as bad as yesterday but close. Oh, so close. The second yank sent tears to her eyes but they didn't fall today.

"Okay, more ice today and take it easy." Chris patted her shoulder and then helped her stand.

"I will." Ava had no plans to do anything other than sit in her recliner, sleep, and maybe write a little if she was lucky.

~

*W*hen she woke that afternoon, the first thing she did was pop more Tylenol. She didn't like feeling like she needed it to get through the day, but that's exactly where she was.

The Tylenol dulled the ache enough that she decided to try writing. She settled into the chair and opened her laptop, but before she dove into her story, she decided to check her mail. Normally an everyday activity, she hadn't done it at all yesterday.

Ava sighed as she read the first email. She was supposed to lead worship practice tonight. Having always loved singing, she had joined the worship team shortly after she and Justin married. And she loved it, but the thought of singing on stage this week with such pain in her neck filled her with fear. She should cancel, say she couldn't make it, but the normal worship leader and the pianist were both out of town. The responsibility for making sure the team practiced and sounded good lay firmly on her shoulders.

She'd have Justin drive her tonight. He'd said he'd be home earlier today. Dropping Kylie off was scary enough but Heidi's home was close so she didn't have to drive far. The church was across town and would require getting on the interstate – not something Ava felt comfortable doing with no movement in her neck. And surely by Sunday the pain would be gone or at least diminished enough that she could function.

With her game plan figured out, Ava finished checking the mail and then loaded her work in progress. The words came easily enough but fatigue hit with them, and by early afternoon, she was fairly certain she had slept more than she had written.

~

"Hey baby, let's get you in the car. You get to come to worship practice with Mommy tonight." Ava forced a cheeriness in her voice that she didn't feel but hoped would relieve any fears that Kylie might be feeling.

Kylie's eyes lit up and she clapped her hands together. "Can we watch you sing?"

"Sure, baby, if it's okay with Daddy." Ava glanced Justin's direction and he nodded.

"Might as well since we are your ride."

"Thank you for this," Ava said lowering her voice so Kylie wouldn't overhear. "I just didn't want to chance anything having to drive so much farther."

"It's my pleasure. I don't need anything happening to you." He planted a quick kiss on her cheek before ushering them out the door.

Ava tried not to grimace during the ride to the church. On one hand, she was glad Justin was driving so she didn't have to move her neck, but he was a much more aggressive driver than she was and he didn't avoid the bumps or slow down on the turns which also aggravated her pain. Relief flooded her when the car stopped and the engine turned off.

"Mommy, come get me," Kylie hollered from behind Justin's seat.

"Baby, I wish I could, but Daddy is going to have to get you today." This was what Ava hated the most - not being able to function normally, not being able to pick up her daughter. "But I'll hold your hand once he gets you down."

"Okay." Resignation filled Kylie's voice, but she didn't fight them.

Justin and Kylie sat dutifully in the front row of the church while Ava led worship. The pain never left, but an odd tingling sensation trickled across her head as she sang the words to God. Perhaps just lifting her praises to God in this way would bring the healing she sought.

CHAPTER 5

*A*va woke even stiffer Friday morning. How was that possible? Shouldn't two adjustments have helped if it was a pinched nerve? Did that mean it was something more serious? Something she should worry about?

Amazed she had been able to sleep in the bed instead of the recliner, Ava braced for the pain as she pushed herself upright. Sure enough, it washed over her, a tidal wave of tightness, stiffness, and the feeling of a knife jabbing into the right side of her neck. It took a moment for the blackness to fade and the room to stay still enough that she could stand.

A shower sounded like the most painful thing on Earth at the moment, but she hadn't taken one yesterday. Two days was her limit. Even after Kylie had been born, she'd snuck into the bathroom and given herself as much of a shower as she could the second day much to the chagrin of the nurse who found her there. She'd taken a tongue lashing and been forced to promise she would call for help next time before she attempted a shower, but at least she had gotten clean. The gritty, slimy feeling had left her hair and taken the constant itch with it. And that was all Ava was hoping for today. Just enough clean to not feel gross.

She peeled off her clothes and stepped into the warm shower. The water pelted her neck but not in a painful way. Washing her hair, on the other hand, nearly brought her to tears. Unable to lean her head back, she backed closer to the shower head and let the water pour down her face. She scrubbed the soap out while trying to stay as still as possible and breathed a sigh of relief when the cleansing process was finished. But drying off was no less painful. Trying to dry her hair without moving her neck proved impossible and she stopped when the pain became unbearable. Her hair wasn't dry – far from it – but it could air dry the rest of the way.

"Mommy!" Kylie's yell came from down the hall. They had taken the railing off her bed a year ago, but she still refused to get up herself.

"Coming," Ava hollered back. Nothing like rushing to get dressed when you could barely move. She pulled on a pair of sweatpants and a loose-fitting shirt before heading down the hallway to Kylie's room. "Morning bug. You ready to get up?"

"Can I stay home with you today, Mommy?" Kylie asked as she sat up and rubbed her eyes. Her little stuffed lamb, once a pure white color but now loved to a dirty beige, was clasped tightly against her chest.

"Not today, baby, but it's Friday, which means tomorrow is Saturday and that's a stay home all day with Mommy day." Ava opened Kylie's drawers and pulled out her clothes for the day.

"Okay, Mommy."

Ava smiled as Kylie followed her downstairs. If only everyone was as accommodating and easy to please as her four-year old.

~

*A*va dropped her keys on the table and sank into the recliner again. The third adjustment had been less painful, but Chris had promised she would have more movement and she still didn't. It still hurt to move her neck and swallow. Something else had to be going on.

As she pulled up her email, a message icon popped across her screen. Results from her x-rays had posted to her health account. Unsure she would understand the medical jargon but curious as to what it might say, she logged in and clicked on the medical record. The report wasn't long, but the words sent a spear of fear into her heart:

Impression: Unremarkable bony structures of the cervical spine. Nonspecific prevertebral soft tissue swelling from the C1 level to the C4 level. Clinical correlation for possible prevertebral infection is recommended. Consider

CT neck with contrast to further evaluate. POSITIVE ALERT The results of this study have been annotated as abnormal in the patient's electronic medical record.

Prevertebral tissue swelling? What did that mean? Possible infection? CT scan? Abnormal? Suddenly, Ava was convinced this was not just a pinched nerve. She grabbed her cell phone and dialed the number to the clinic. Hopefully she hadn't made things worse by waiting so long to be seen. It was only two days. Surely two days wouldn't matter.

"Family health center, how may I direct your call?"

"I need to set an appointment to be seen," Ava said.

The woman transferred her to the right department and Ava rattled off the details of the x-ray report.

"I can get you in Monday morning with Dr. Stedman but that's the earliest appointment I have," the woman on the other end said apologetically.

"That's okay. I'll take it." But Ava wasn't going to wait another two days to be seen. Not with the words abnormal hanging over her head. She might have to sit there for hours, but her clinic had an Urgent Care department. At least she would get seen today. She tucked her laptop into her bag, grabbed her keys, and headed out for the second time.

The Urgent Care department was surprisingly slow when Ava arrived, and after being checked in, she was whisked quickly back into the triage room and then down the hall to a more permanent room. A nurse peppered her with questions before promising to return shortly with the doctor.

Ava sat in the chair and tried not to let fear overtake her. A few minutes later, a large, friendly black woman entered.

"Ava, I'm Dr. Jensen. I've looked over your results and I'm lining up a CT scan immediately. It may be nothing but infections in the neck are never something to mess with. Okay?"

"Whatever you suggest. I just want the pain to go away."

"We do need you to get on the bed. Erica needs to put an IV in because this CT will use an iodine contrast. Can you lie down?"

Ava sat on the edge of the bed. "Lying down is a little tough, but I'll try."

The doctor pushed a button to bring the head of the bed up so that it wasn't as much of an incline and Ava gratefully leaned back. The position still wasn't completely comfortable but it was much better than laying flat.

"All right, Erica will get you set up and then someone from the CT unit will be in to get you. I'll be back once I have results."

"Thank you."

Ava watched as the nurse inserted a needle into her veins and began to draw blood out. Normally, she hated having blood drawn but the pain was so minor compared to the aching in her neck that she didn't even care. After filling four vials, the nurse plugged in the piece that would attach to the IV and left the room.

Ava pulled out her cell phone and opened her book app. She couldn't write, but maybe she could pass the time reading. She rarely got to anymore since most of her free time was spent writing.

"Ava Miller?"

Ava glanced over at the door where a young woman stood with a wheelchair. "That's me." The woman helped get her situated in the wheelchair and then pushed her out the back doors of the clinic.

"I know it seems odd, but the CT scanners are housed in these mobile units. Don't worry though, they work just the same."

Ava would have nodded if she were able but as the statement didn't appear to require an answer, she didn't give one.

The woman maneuvered the wheelchair onto a ramp and then pressed a button to raise the ramp. When it stopped, she manually lifted the metallic closure and the interior of the trailer was exposed. It looked like a miniature lab with another technician manning a computer just outside of the white CT machine.

"Have you ever had a CT scan with contrast?" the technician asked her.

"I don't think so." Ava wasn't even sure she'd ever had a CT before much less with contrast.

"Are you allergic to iodine?"

"Not that I know of." What happened if she was?

Visions of her coding or going into some short of shock filled her mind and she closed her eyes to force them away. Sometimes having the imagination of a writer was a curse as much as a blessing.

"Can you lie back?" the woman asked.

"Not without help," Ava replied and the two flanked her and helped her lie back.

"Okay, now when the iodine hits, you're going to feel a warm sensation. It might even feel like you've wet yourself, but don't worry that's normal."

Ava wasn't sure how that could be normal but she said nothing.

"Be sure to keep your eyes closed throughout the procedure and there's a few times I'm going to ask you not to swallow."

No worries there. Swallowing was extremely painful and she avoided it at all costs. The bed she was on moved and Ava shut her eyes. A few minutes later, the CT scan was done. The technicians helped her back up and the woman who wheeled her out wheeled her back to her room.

Before climbing back in the bed, Ava grabbed her computer and placed it beside her along with her phone. She should have brought her charger in, but she couldn't imagine she would be here much longer.

She was wrong. It was an hour later when the nurse finally returned. "Looks like I need a little more blood and then you need to get this antibiotic which takes about half an hour to administer."

"Antibiotic? So, it is an infection then?"

The nurse appeared thrown by the question. "Dr. Jensen hasn't been back in yet?"

"No one's been in for over an hour. I was beginning to think you'd forgotten about me."

"No, we haven't. I'll get you started and then check in with Dr. Jensen." The nurse filled a few more vials with blood and then fiddled with the IV plug for a minute until she appeared satisfied the IV was hooked up correctly. "Back in a bit," she said as she exited the room.

Ava sighed. An infection wasn't great news, but antibiotics generally cured them and at least it might mean faster relief for her neck.

"Oh good, Erica got you set up," Dr. Jensen said as she re-entered the room. "So, it does look like you have an infection in your neck. I'm glad you came in when you did. We don't want an infection like this getting into your bloodstream."

"How would I know if it got into my bloodstream?"

"You would probably have severe chills or fever. If you have any of those signs, you need to go straight to the ER, not here, do you understand?"

"Yes ma'am."

"I'm prescribing you a strong antibiotic that you need to take for ten days along with a muscle relaxer and some pain medicine that you can take as needed. I want you to set a follow-up appointment for a week from now to make sure everything is improving."

"I can do that." Ava would do just about anything if it would lessen the pain she was feeling.

"Good. Erica will be back shortly with your discharge paperwork and your pharmacy papers. I hope you feel better soon."

So did Ava.

CHAPTER 6

*A*va woke with a start to the sun coming in her window. Ten am? How had she slept so long? Even though Saturday was a sleep in day, Kylie never let her sleep past eight. Justin must have gotten her before she could wake Ava up.

Ava tested her neck. It was definitely still stiff, but the throbbing seemed a little less today. Or was that just wishful thinking? Maybe, but it also hurt less to swallow and that she was not making up. It was the first time in days that swallowing didn't feel like someone squeezing her throat. Perhaps the medicine was working.

As she went to sit up though, the pain struck anew. Not as bad as yesterday but definitely not healed. Baby steps. She would need to do baby steps. Ava rolled to her left side and then pushed herself up that way. Less pain, but the world still tilted for a minute. When it stopped, she continued into the bathroom and dressed for the day.

"How you feeling today, honey?" Justin asked as she stepped into the kitchen.

"Better. Not great yet, but better." She tilted her head but there was still little movement.

"Mommy, Daddy and I let you sleep in. Weren't we good?" Kylie asked appearing over the back of the couch.

"You were very good, baby. Mommy thanks you. Sleep is important for Mommy to heal. And so is breakfast." Ava poured herself a bowl of cereal and then a cup of coffee.

"We can just stay home today, right Mommy?"

"We can, but maybe you can let Mommy get a little writing done? I've been so tired that I haven't written much at all this week."

"Sure, I can do that."

Ava smiled at her daughter. Even when her life was turned upside down, she managed to keep a smile on her face and find the joy in the small things in life. If only adults could live life more like children.

In her pocket, her cell phone buzzed and Ava pulled it out curious as to who would be calling. "Joyce? What can I do for you?" Joyce was the pianist and the boss of the worship team as far as Ava was concerned.

"I heard about your neck. If you need to take tomorrow to sleep, John can lead for you."

"Thank you. I started medication last night so I'm hopeful it will feel better, but if it's not better tonight, I promise I'll call you and John." Ava knew she probably should stay home, but she felt closest to God when she was on stage singing, and she hated giving that up. Unless her neck worsened today, she was sure she could make it through the three hours of church anyway.

"You don't think staying home would be a good idea?" Justin asked her after she ended the call.

"It might, but I feel like God asked me to lead for the same reason He asked me to write. I always feel like there's something He wants me to say. If I get nothing by tonight and the pain is any worse, I'll surrender."

Justin shot her a look full of disbelief, but he didn't argue. After five years of marriage, he knew when to push and when to step back, and Ava loved him even more for that. She planted a kiss on his cheek on her way to the sink where she deposited her dishes. Hopefully she would feel up to washing them later.

∾

"*H*ey sleepyhead, you do any work anymore?" Ava opened her eyes to see Gen standing over her. What time was it? Her neck felt stiff, but maybe that was just from the uncomfortable position of the recliner. "Sorry, Gen, I was working, but I guess I dozed off." She turned her wrist to see her watch and her eyes widened. It was nearly six? She'd slept through lunch and almost through dinner?

"I can see that. I brought some Chinese if you feel up to it."

"Mongolian Beef?" Ava asked hopefully. It was her favorite and Gen knew it.

"Of course. I would never show up without your favorite. I also have some Orange Chicken for Justin and some Sweet and Sour Chicken for little miss Kylie." She flashed a smile at Kylie who sat on the couch watching something on YouTube.

"You didn't let her watch TV all afternoon, did you?" Ava asked Justin as she righted the recliner and pushed herself up. She really needed her neck to heal so she could back to her routine. Two hours of TV was all she ever allowed Kylie and that was only on rare occasions.

"Relax, we just got back from the park. When I heard you snoring, I figured we could sneak out and let you get some rest." He shot her a teasing smirk before running off into the dining room.

"I don't snore," Ava shot after him, but she wondered if this medicine wasn't affecting her in some way. Twice, she had woken herself up with some noise from her throat before sleep overtook her again.

"How is the neck today?" Gen asked. She grabbed a few bowls from Ava's cupboard and some forks before continuing into the dining room.

"Better than yesterday, but not as good as I'd hoped. Oh, I need to tell Chris I can't come in Monday after all. The doctor said no more adjustments until the infection is gone."

"Don't worry, I'll tell Chris, but did they tell you where this infection came from?" Gen set the bowls down and doled out the forks.

Ava shrugged and scooted back a chair. "She said a sinus infection, but I didn't even know I had one."

"Well, you did have that really nasty cold thing last week that you swore was allergies. It could have been a sinus infection with as much as you blew your nose." Gen dished up Kylie's plate and put the appropriate container in front of each of the adults before taking her own seat.

"I suppose that's possible." Ava had forgotten all about the allergy troubles from the week before, but now that she thought back on them – they were worse than they ever had been. Generally, she only needed her Flonase in the morning to feel better, but that week she'd had to take her Flonase in the morning and afternoon as well as a Zyrtec in the morning. Could that have been a sinus infection instead of just allergies?

"Can we pray for Mommy to feel better?" Kylie asked.

"Of course baby, why don't you pray?" Ava smiled at her daughter before closing her eyes.

"Lord, thank you for sending Aunt Gen with the food and thank you for the nice day today so Daddy and I could have fun at the park. Please heal Mommy so she can have fun with us again too. Amen."

The adults all echoed the Amen, but the mood around the table had shifted. What if the medicine didn't work? What if Ava had to deal with this neck pain and fatigue forever? Though she knew she was blessed, at that moment all the blessings she had taken for granted flashed in her vision - the days she had woken pain free and not thanked God, the times she had been frustrated that Kylie wanted her attention when she wanted to do something else. Had this happened to make Ava take a long look at her life?

She knew the answer before she asked the question. And with that answer came the one she had been waiting on all day – the words she should share tomorrow. Ava had no idea who needed them, but they were so clear in her head that she knew they must be from God. So, neither pain nor stiffness nor exhaustion mattered. She would be on the stage tomorrow and she would share His message.

CHAPTER 7

"*H*ow are you feeling?" John asked as she stepped on the stage the next morning. He was readying the mics which was supposed to be her job as leader, but she knew that he was doing it out of kindness for her and she thanked him with a smile.

"Not completely better, but good enough to be here. Thank you for asking and thank you for helping set up."

"My pleasure. I know how pain can affect your life."

As he moved the stands to the front, his situation hit her. She'd known he had chronic pain problems, but until this week, she'd really had no idea how that must feel. Now she did, and she would never forget it. He would be on her mind every morning in prayer and she would remember to ask how she could help him in the future.

"You feeling up to leading this?" Joyce asked as she took her place behind the piano.

"I am, and I have something I need to share. Can I talk before one of the songs?"

"Sure." Joyce pulled out the order of worship and they scanned it together. "Probably best here before Reckless Love or just after."

"I'll do it after since John is starting Reckless Love." Ava didn't really care where it went in the message. She just knew it had to be there.

The rest of the musicians and singers found their places on stage and the team ran through the songs. Then the pastor joined them on stage and they prayed for the message and for healing of Ava's neck. She hadn't taken her muscle relaxers because they made her drowsy and she could feel the heaviness in her neck creeping in already, but Ava knew she would make it through the next three hours.

As the rest of the team wandered off to use the bathroom or grab a coffee, Ava grabbed her Bible. She wanted to read something about God always being there, but she hadn't been in the Word enough lately to know which passage she wanted. After a quick Google search, she found a few verses she thought would do and when she opened her Bible to Philippians 4, she knew she had hit gold. The words not only resonated with her, but they felt right.

She closed her eyes and sent a silent prayer heavenward. "Thank you, Lord for opening my eyes this week. Thank you for making me focus on you more. Please give me the words to speak this morning that you want me to say. Shine through me today and use me as you need to."

At five minutes to nine the band began playing. Ava grabbed her Bible and opened it up to the right page. When the clock at the back showed ten seconds left, she stepped up to the mic. "Good morning church. I'm so glad you could be with us today. I'm Ava Miller, and I'll be your worship leader. Before we sing, I'd like to share some scripture with you, so if you're able, will you stand and join me in the reading of God's word? I'm reading from The Message Bible because I really like how they put it in easy to read terms, and I'm reading Philippians 4:4-10."

She took a deep breath before reading aloud the verses. "'Celebrate God all day, every day. I mean, revel in Him! Make it as clear as you can to all you meet that you're on their side, working with them and not against them. Help them see that the Master is about to arrive. He could show up any minute!

"'Don't fret or worry. Instead of worrying, pray. Let petitions and praises shape your worries into prayers, letting God know your concerns. Before you know it, a sense of God's wholeness, everything coming together for good, will come and settle you down. It's wonderful what happens when Christ displaces worry at the center of your life.

"'Summing it all up, friends, I'd say you'll do best by filling your minds and meditating on things true, noble, reputable, authentic, compelling, gracious – the best, not the worst; the beautiful, not the ugly; things to praise, not things to curse. Put into practice what you learned from me, what you heard and saw and realized. Do that, and God, who makes everything work together, will work you into his most excellent harmonies.' Amen?"

"Amen," the crowd responded and Ava led them in prayer before the singing began. Just like at practice on Thursday, Ava felt tingling in her head as she sang the praises to God. Maybe it was all in her head, but she felt like she was receiving healing as she sang on the platform, and before she knew it, they were ending Reckless Love.

Ava closed her eyes as she envisioned the words she would say. The music softened behind her. "Before we sing this next song, I need to share something that God laid on my heart last night. See, I wasn't sure I was going to be here this morning. Earlier this week, I woke up with a soreness in my neck and by that afternoon, I couldn't move it. I thought it was just a pinched nerve, so I went to a chiropractor who thankfully sent me for x-rays before he adjusted me. Then I had another adjustment the next day and another on Friday and when I got home on Friday, the results from the x-ray were in my email inbox, and they were abnormal. So, I went to Urgent Car and after a CT scan, they found I didn't have a pinched nerve but an infection in my neck." She pointed to the spot on her neck and saw the reaction from the crowd. Some of the women had covered their mouths with their hands, but all eyes appeared firmly on her.

"And God reminded me that sin is a lot like my pain. It sneaks up on us. We do one thing thinking it's not so bad and then another and then another and before we know it, we are mired down in sin. But God is also like my doctor. When I got there Friday night, she didn't say 'Why didn't you come in Wednesday when this first happened?' No, she said 'I'm so glad you came in when you did.' And God is like that too. He's not looking to condemn us but to save us, and like we just sang, he leaves the ninety-nine to go find the one. To go find you. So, if you're here today and you don't know God because you think you've done something so terrible that He could never love you – You're wrong! And if you've distanced yourself from God because you've been mired down in sin and you think you've done something so awful that He could never forgive you – You're wrong! Because God is like that doctor. He is just waiting for us to come to Him and when we do, He doesn't say we should have come sooner. He says 'I'm glad you came when you did.' Will you join us as we sing this last song?"

If Ava thought she had felt power in the church before that song, it was nothing like the power she felt as they sang the last song. The tingling in her head was almost overpowering, but for a moment, she felt no pain and no stiffness.

"God really used you today," Joyce said as the team gathered their items together at the end of the service. "That was exactly the right thing to say and the perfect analogy."

"I agree. I was almost in tears," Alanna said coming up behind her.

"Thank you. I've never been sure I hear God speaking to me, but when that came into my head last night, I knew it had to be Him."

"Excuse me."

Ava looked up to see a man she didn't know coming up the stairs of the stage. He was an older gentleman, probably in his late sixties or seventies with thinning white hair. "Yes, sir?"

"Can you tell me what you read today?"

"Philippians 4:4-10," Ava replied.

"Thank you," he said as he scribbled something down on a paper. "Those were exactly the words I needed to hear today along with what you said at the end."

Ava blinked at him a moment, amazed. "Thank you," she managed. She'd believed God had given her the words to say, but she didn't usually have people come and tell her they were touched.

"Seems like God had a plan for you this week," Justin said as he joined her at the base of the stage.

"Yeah, I guess so. Who would have thought a disabling neck pain would have such a profound effect?"

"I stopped questioning God's motives a long time ago," Justin said with a laugh. He took her hand as they walked down the hallway to the childcare center to retrieve Kylie.

Before they reached their car in the parking lot, three more people approached Ava thanking her for her words. Ava nodded and smiled and said 'you're welcome' with each one, but she knew she had done nothing. It had all been God.

"Mommy, is your neck better today?" Kylie asked as Ava buckled her into the car.

"It is baby, and though it's not completely healed yet, I have a feeling it will be soon."

"I know it will be," Kylie said with a smile. "God told me this morning you would be better. He just needed you to see. I thought that was silly because it was your neck that hurt and not your eyes, but do you see, Mommy?"

"I do now, bug. I do now." Ava leaned in and kissed her daughter's forehead. As she shut Kylie's door, she turned her face to the sky. "Thank you, Lord, for helping me see."

The End!

AUTHOR'S NOTE

*F*irst off, let me say how glad I am that you read this book. I originally wanted to release this at the beginning of May, but then I got a BookBub for The Cowboy's Reality Bride, and I put this book on hold for a few weeks to try for a run at the USA Today list.

Unfortunately, I didn't make the list and by the time I got back to the story, I had lost my groove, so it took a little longer for me to finish. Around the middle of the month, I had a crazy medical experience. If you are curious as to what, be sure to click for the bonus epilogue as I wrote it into Ava's story. It's my way of saying thank you for taking a chance on me and my books.

And if you've enjoyed reading this author's note so far (and really, how could you not?) I am offering, for today only, a page where you can sign up for my weekly newsletter for the low, low price of absolutely nothing.

Included in this weekly newsletter is many wonderful

things like pictures of my adorable children, chances to win awesome prizes, new releases and sales I might be holding, great books from other authors, and anything else that strikes my fancy and that I think you would enjoy.

Even better, I solemnly swear to only send out one newsletter a week (usually on Tuesday unless life gets in the way which with three kids it usually does). I will not spam you, sell your email address to solicitors or anyone else, or any of those other terrible things.

Join me here and receive the free short story as my thank-you gift for choosing to hang out with me. It's fun and entertaining. I promise.

Prayers and blessings,

Lorana

NOT READY TO SAY GOODBYE YET?

The Producer's Unlikely Bride is the sixth book in the multi-author Blushing Bride series, but my second (or third if you count the bonus short story, The Reality Bride's Baby). While each book written by a different author in the series will be a stand alone, I have decided to make mine a series. If you are reading on Amazon, the numbers may look confusing, but just know that my books will twine together. You don't have to have read The Cowboy's Reality Bride for this book to make sense, but if you have, you will have a better understanding of Justin and Peter.

With that in mind, the next book in the Blushing Bride series will be The Cop's Fiery Bride. I decided to give Cassidy her own story.

The book will open after Cassidy returns home from being on the show. Obviously she didn't find love, but what she has found is a ton of guys trying to court her and massive teasing from her fellow firefighters.

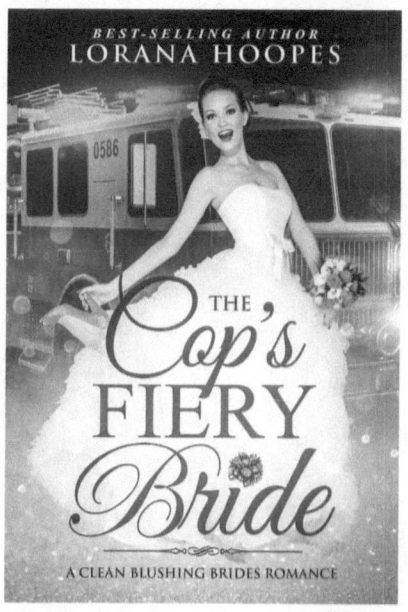

The Cop's Fiery Bride

A firefighter who just wants to get back to work.

Cassidy is glad to be back home after the reality dating show, but she did not expect so many men to be reaching out to her. Nor did she expect the teasing from her fellow firefighters. When she sees something at a fire that makes no sense, will she be able to convince anyone to take her seriously?

He's a cop who's avoided Cassidy as much as possible.

But not because he doesn't like her. Unfortunately Cassidy reminds Jordan of a painful past. However, when she sees something odd during a fire, he is forced to spend time with her to figure out what it all means

Be sure to pre-order The Cop's Fiery Bride

THE STORY DOESN'T END!

You've met a few people and fallen in love....

I bet you're wondering how you can meet everyone else.

Star Lake Series:
When Love Returns
Once Upon a Star
Love Conquers All
Heartbeats Series:
Where It All Began
The Power of Prayer
When Hearts Collide
A Past Forgiven
Sweet Billionaires Series:
The Billionaire's Secret
Brush with a Billionaire
The Billionaire's Christmas Miracle
The Billionaire's Cowboy Groom

The Lawkeepers series:
Lawfully Matched
Lawfully Justified
The Scarlet Wedding
Lawfully Redeemed
Lawfully Pursued
Stand alones:
The Still Small Voice
Love Renewed
Blushing Brides Series:
The Cowboy's Reality Bride
The Reality Bride's Baby
The Producer's Unlikely Bride
Ava's Blessing in Disguise
The Cop's Fiery Bride
Her children's early reader chapter book series:
The Wishing Stone #1: Dangerous Dinosaur
The Wishing Stone #2: Dragon Dilemma
The Wishing Stone #3: Mesmerizing Mermaids
The Wishing Stone #4: Pyramid Puzzles
The Wishing Stone Inspirations #1: Mary's Miracle
To see a list of all her books

authorloranahoopes.com
loranahoopes@gmail.com

DISCUSSION QUESTIONS

1. What was your favorite scene in the book? What made it your favorite?

2. Did you have a favorite line in the book? What do you think made it so memorable?

3. Who was your favorite character in the book and why?

4. Ava turned away relationships searching for perfection. What perfect goal do you have that maybe needs to be thought out again?

· · ·

5. What do you think would be the hardest part about being on a reality dating show?

6. What did you learn about God from reading this book?

7. How can you use that knowledge in your life from now on?

8. What can you take away from Ava's and Justin's relationship?

9. What do you think would make the story even better?

ABOUT THE AUTHOR

Lorana Hoopes is an inspirational author originally from Texas but now living in the PNW with her husband and three children. When not writing, she can be seen kickboxing at the gym, singing, or acting on stage. One day, she hopes to retire from teaching and write full time.

www.ingramcontent.com/pod-product-compliance
Lightning Source LLC
Chambersburg PA
CBHW050458260626
47157CB00004B/1103